CONTENTS

TO BE FOREVER

BY ANGEL SANTIAGO

FIRST EDITION: May 2019

Cover Illustration by Stephen Green

Internal Illustrations by Logan Slominski

Edited by Rosalind Stanley

ISBN: 978-1-0966-0080-0 (Paperback)

*To my friends, family, all the people
I've met, the universe...*

and Mill Mountain Coffee.

*I could have never lived the beautiful, interesting
experiences I needed to live to write this without
all of you.*

Angel Santiago

As is a tale, so is life: not how long it is, but how good it is, is what matters. - Seneca

DAY 0:

THE FATEFUL ENCOUNTER

Time: the currency of experience. The only thing we will never get back once it is spent.

I lay in the verdant field, surrounded by the sweet aromas of flowers, and with the warmth of the sun acting as my blanket. In this moment, I was struck by that omnipotent, interminable truth which had brought an end to so many great kings and queens and to all who have inhabited the world. I knew that at some point it would be over; I would have to wake up from this serene dream, once the time afforded to me dwindled to the final tick of breath, and return once again to that boundless, silent oblivion that is as familiar as it is foreign.

A loud, gurgling yelp came from farther down in the field. I shifted my eyes from the sky to a fox proudly displaying a rabbit caught between its jaws. The rabbit twitched a few times before it fell, limp. The fox and I looked intently at one another, before it tilted its snout up triumphantly, as if to signify that it noticed me, and then it trotted into the forest. I wondered if the fox knew that it had taken the life of another being; foxes are quite intelligent, after all. Before the rabbit had been swept away with no say in the matter, I am sure it had spent the day much as I had. Like the rabbit's, my time would end too—someday. I shut my eyes slowly and sighed.

"Your father is dead!" my mother had cried out one bright, *spring morning many months ago. "...he is not with us anymore,"* she *said, weeping.*

His hands were as cold as the frost in winter; squeezing them caused a sharp pain in my own. I wanted him to wake up. I wished hopelessly, with tears in my eyes, that I could evade Death's omnipotent hold over me.

Death made no sense to me. It held all of us within its grasp and seemed to pull many away from this world on a mere whim.

I was silent as my mother mourned my father's unexpected end. He was a happy, proud man, a good man—one who didn't deserve to be taken away so early.

Now, the memory of a myth that my father had read to me as a child stirred me from my relaxed state—there lived a wise man known simply as The Sage. His origins were clouded in mystery, but his capacity was not. He was a man so wise that he could turn paupers into kings and idiots into wise men. Of course, The Sage did not appear to just anyone; being worthy of The Sage's counsel was decided by two factors—your dream and your soul.

I had been intrigued by this story ever since my father's passing, but I knew I would never meet such a figure. I was certainly not a noble soul, and besides, The Sage, like the legends that surrounded him, only existed in storybooks. With all my heart, I hoped that if such a figure did exist, that he would grant me the one thing I wanted above all else: eternal life.

Standing up, I breathed in one last breath of the fresh air that permeated the meadow. I had the sudden feeling that the branches and vines around me were beckoning me deeper into the forest. So I walked, my curiosity growing, pressing me to continue. Part of me worried that I would be alone with nature forever if I did not begin to move back towards town, but I decided to set my fears aside and sate my inquisitive disposition.

Sunlight radiated through the canopy onto one little, out-of-place cottage, surrounded by plants of many kinds. A large tree branch suddenly fell to the forest floor behind me. I was not especially superstitious, but it appeared that nature would allow me only one course of action. I stepped slowly towards the enigmatic home.

The cottage was simple, yet magnificent, composed of light gray stone that shone brilliantly and beautiful scarlet shingles. The door appeared ancient, with a handle made from a thick vine, and covered in moss in different shades of green. The moss itself seemed to be pulsing, as if welcoming me.

"Who could possibly live out here in the woods?" I asked myself. And how had I never seen this house? I had travelled through the forest countless times. Maybe a lumberjack lived here, or some sort of witch doctor.

I took a deep breath and banged my knuckles on the mystifying door. Before I could knock a second time, the door opened slowly, and a bold voice began to speak.

"Yes, come in. I've been waiting for you."

I was as surprised as I was fearful. As I walked into the cottage, my eyes settled on the owner of this intriguing place.

"I am curious. What brings you to my humble home today?"

Humble was the last word I would have used to describe the interior of this incongruous building. The room I had entered was as large itself as the entire cottage appeared to be from the outside. I saw hallways, too, that sprawled in all directions to other rooms. What I had first called a cottage now seemed a palace.

"I don't know why I am here today, honestly; I was just enjoying a walk in the woods, and I had never seen your house before," I said to the man nervously.

The man in front of me didn't seem any older than about

4

forty. Dark brown hair covered his head, with touches of gray at the roots. A tattered, ocean-blue robe shrouded his body; from its condition, I assumed it had been in his ownership for years. Underneath his robe, he wore a speckled, dark-green shirt tucked into worn, cream-colored pants and shin-high boots that seemed to have seen more adventures than I had ever even read about in my whole life. "Well, I know why you are here today. I just decided to ask you in order to make your experience here a little less eerie."

I was awe-struck and a little bit skeptical. No mortal man could possibly know the reason I was at his house if I did not even know! I saw again the mystical quality of this misleadingly un-suspecting building, though, and realized that I was dealing with someone a bit more than just a mortal man.

My mother had always told me that you could tell a lot about a person by their eyes, and I believed it now. The man's dominating eyes roiled with sepia and amber. Peering into them for too long brought forth an unnerving feeling that forced me to glance down often while I was talking to him.

"What do you want most, more than anything else?" the mysterious man asked.

"Why do you ask?" It was odd to hear such an intimate question from someone I barely knew.

"you'll learn more about a person by what they want, not by what they say," the man said. I shrugged. No real harm could come out of divulging my desire to this man, no matter how strange he seemed to be.

"Well, I have always wanted to live forever." I could not lie about that; living for all eternity and forever experiencing what-ever I wished was my most powerful desire.

"Ha! Is that truly what you wish to have, more than any-thing else?" Irritated, I wondered what right this man had to laugh at my greatest wish. "Are you sure you do not desire infinite riches? Maybe you would like to become a king? You might at least wish to have a large home or many possessions; why do you wish to have eternal life?" he asked, this time in a genuinely curious manner.

"I enjoy spending my time as I see fit, but I recognized early on that you only possess a finite amount of time. I have witnessed death before; it seemed so terrifying to *not be*. I do not care about fame or fortune. Those do not interest me in the way that time does. If I possessed infinite time, I would be the richest man in the world in humans' most valuable resource," I said. I expected this curious man to accept my explanation and understand why I valued the idea of eternal life so much, but it was quite the opposite. The man let out a roaring and booming laugh that sounded like waves crashing against a seaside precipice. Now I was angry. Before I could begin to yell, though, the man's lighthearted demeanor vanished. His expression grew dour. His gaze seemed to pierce deeply into the content of my character. I was forced to bow my head; his eyes exuded an intensity I had never felt before.

"You haven't figured out who I am yet, have you?" he asked in a serious tone.

I did not respond.

"I know you enjoy reading; have you never read the myths of the The Sage?"

The way he spoke the name told me that he was claiming to be the one person who could bring me what I had thought to be imaginary. The claim was ridiculous. Unless it were true.

"You...there is no way."

"Come. Let us take a walk through my home while we talk about what you are here for today. You'll believe me before too long." The man motioned towards a hallway on the other side of the foyer.

I nodded my head and began to follow the man I was coming to think of as The Sage around his vast home.

Inspecting his living room with more focus, I saw that the walls were painted a light russet color. Flowers hung from the ceiling in brilliant golden pots. Shelves were lined with a superb array of different trinkets and items. Exotic herbs, small stuffed animals, chalices, time-keepers—each item must have possessed an incredible and unique history.

"You are quite the curious fellow, aren't you?"

I snapped out of my reverie. "You just..."

Before I could finish my sentence, The Sage spoke again.

"I have collected a great deal over the years."

Stroking his beard, The Sage turned to me and smiled warmly. We continued through his unassuming palace.

The hallway we entered stretched far, so far, in fact, that I had trouble making out the distant kitchen. An enthralling suit of blinding ivory armor stood close to the middle of the hallway. It held both a spear and shield in a stoic fashion. The armor was not ornately decorated, but its simplicity made it all the more remarkable. As I investigated its intimidating two-faced helmet, it shifted to glance in my direction. The sudden movement frightened me, and I fell back onto my rear.

"Did something scare you?" The Sage asked, laughing.

"That armor! It moved!" I gasped, getting back to my feet.

"That is no suit of armor, Adventurer.... Well, he *is* a suit of armor, but that is not the point. His name is Janus. Janus and I have been friends for years now. I give him a place to stay, and in return, he guards me and my humble little cottage. Now, if only he could *gard-en*—he would truly earn his keep then!" As The Sage laughed at his own little joke, Janus glanced over and then assumed his original position. Janus' subtle glance led me to believe that he was not amused by The Sage's eccentric sense of humor.

We reached the kitchen sooner than I expected. Various pots and pans hung from the ceiling above a small black stove. The Sage took a seat at the kitchen table, which, like most of the other objects in The Sage's home, had an unearthly quality to it. "Take a seat!" he beckoned. "I'm sure you are hungry."

Sitting at the table, I realized that everything surrounding me was a relic of the past. Each item tethered us to another period of history, an antiquated reality that had long been forgotten.

"So," The Sage began.

"Yes?" I did not know what to talk about.

"Having conversations with people becomes rather dull when you already know what the other person is going to say,"

The Sage said, yawning.

"So why bother talking at all?" I asked, agitated.

"Because that is how time works, Adventurer. It is impossible to move forward without action. I've gotten used to having conversations of which I already know the outcome. What is funny about life is that most of it is predictable. Even to someone like you." I could sense The Sage growing more pensive as we spoke. I scowled. "There is no reason for you to frown, although it was meant to occur. You see how this can get difficult?" he finished with good humor.

I wondered how a being as wise and powerful as The Sage could spend so much time laughing.

"I laugh because I see it all, Adventurer: the past, the future, your thoughts, the thoughts of everyone around you. Nothing can come as a surprise, so the only thing left to do is laugh."

I fell back into my seat, astonished by his clairvoyance. "So, why do you do what you do, Sage?" The Sage's expression turned serious once again. "Most of life is predictable, yes. But there are certain points where great changes may take place. Changes that even I cannot see. Most of these points in time, 'forks in the road,' for lack of a better phrase, remain unutilized. The pauper with a propensity for business remains a pauper—without a little push. The natural-born leader who loves his compatriots more than himself remains a mere citizen—until he is given direction. These forks in the road...I give them the choice of one road over another."

Yawning, The Sage served both of us some tomato soup.

His soup was some of the best I had ever had. The flavors of the tomato blended perfectly with the eclectic blend of spices that floated throughout the heavenly liquid.

"So that is what I am? A fork in the road?"

"Well, no. You are a person. Calling you a fork in the road was creating a metaphor," The Sage clarified, slurping his own soup right out of the bowl.

"Well, in the metaphorical sense, if I am a fork in the road, you know all that is going to happen when you give me eternal life?" I felt uneasy.

"Yes," The Sage answered, continuing to work on his soup.

"Well?" It was difficult to comprehend this man's omniscience, especially considering the fact that I could not even begin to imagine my own future.

"No one enjoys spoiling a good book, Adventurer. You will just have to live your life in order to see where it will take you. Like I said before, you possess foresight inferior to mine but superior to most. Like any skill, though, it must be cultivated. We all go into the world blind, that is certain. Most just choose to remain so."

I thought about what The Sage had said, but my future remained uncertain and formless in my mind.

"Seven days," The Sage said, finishing his soup sloppily.

"Seven days?"

"Every person I have chosen has had to prove his or her worth to me, one way or another. You are no exception."

"What will that entail?"

"Come."

The Sage led me out of the kitchen and up a wooden spiral staircase. Our boots made high-pitched clacking noises as we continued up the steps. Each click and clack increased the suspense that I felt, waiting to hear what task The Sage would give me. I was not weak, but neither was I built like a warrior. Portraits of dragons and other fantastic creatures were prevalent in The Sage's house; if The Sage was real, wasn't it possible that these creatures were real, too? And if they were, would I be expected to defend myself against one? My constitution was certainly not robust enough to fight with a dragon, let alone vanquish one. I had never even held a sword in my life. My mind raced as we finally reached our destination—an observatory. Above us, I could see straight to the twilit sky. As I looked around the room, I noticed a small, golden telescope, as well a plainly decorated table with two stools. On top of the table sat a humble teapot and two exquisite teacups.

"I hope you like mint tea," said The Sage.

As he already knew the answer, I did not bother to respond. I sat down and commented on the disparity between the teacups and the teapot: "Sage, why such a plain pot to complement your elegant cups?"

"The original teapot broke some time ago, so I went back to using this one." The Sage grabbed the teapot off the table and held it up. I could see it had been well used. "This pot is actually better than the fancy one that came with the cups, but you wouldn't be able to tell from its appearance. Appearances, Adventurer—don't be deceived by them."

I nodded my head.

"Ah, I love mint tea. So refreshing on a day like this," The Sage sighed as he sipped.

"So, what will I have to do to get what I seek?" I asked The Sage again in a frustrated tone.

"You wish to have eternal life, but you are too impatient for me to finish my tea?" The Sage laughed. As I huffed in response, The Sage's face lit up. "That will be it. Yes, that will do just fine," he murmured, as if he'd come to some sort of realization. "Patience, Adventurer," he said, responding to my puzzled look. "That is what you will have to master before I give you what you seek."

I remained quiet so as not to anger him.

"You are learning," he remarked. "This task should not be too difficult. In fact, I think it will suit you quite well." I waited again for The Sage to speak. "I can see that you feel uncomfortable having to wait." He found a burlap bag that was no bigger than the palm of his hand on the shelf next to the telescope. "Take these seeds and this map. You will plant the seeds from the bag at the location on the map and tend to them every day—after twilight," The Sage explained, pointing to a black X on the map. "If you fail or forget to tend the plant for just one day, it will wither and die, and your chances of gaining eternal life will wither away, as well."

I nodded my head.

"If you can successfully travel to and from the tree and take care of it for the next seven days, I will present myself to you once again with the knowledge that you seek." The Sage remained stoic as he spoke.

"And if I should need help?" I asked.

"That is for you to figure out, Adventurer." The Sage grinned then whispered an incantation. I felt an odd tingling sensation splash over my body like warm water. "I have cast a spell over your eyes and mouth. The tree you are about to plant usually remains invisible. You will now see it as clearly as you see me—once it grows, of course."

"You cast a spell over my mouth as well?" I interrupted.

"Patience," The Sage said, leering at me and smiling. "You may not speak of my existence or the reason for your journey. Well, I should say you *cannot* speak of those things. The magic I have cast will speak for you, should you forget."

I looked at the cracked floors of the observatory and then looked at The Sage again. "I am going back home, and I really enjoy travelling." I put my hand to my mouth in surprise and felt my lips. The magic had worked. The Sage finished his cup of tea and sighed.

"I once brought a boy into this house, a boy very much like you. I sent him off on a journey, one vastly different from the one you are about to undertake. When the boy came back, he told me that he'd told one of his closest friends about me. Soon enough, that boy's friend told his friends, and those friends told their friends, and finally, here we are—I have turned into a legend. I cannot be too angry, though. He was just a boy and boys don't tend to keep their mouths fastened as they should. I've noticed that the magic works better than instruction alone." The Sage poured himself another cup of mint tea. I waited eagerly to hear what else he had to say. "Yes?" I didn't speak.

Finally, The Sage laughed and said, "You mustn't always wait patiently, though. Go on! It's approaching dinnertime, and I have already fed you once. I will show you to the door." The Sage set his teacup down and made his way to the spiral staircase. As we left the observatory, I tilted my head back and looked up at the star-covered sky.

Seven days, I thought.

We were now at the doorway to this extraordinary house once again.

"Once you have tended to the tree on the seventh day, my cottage will appear to you once more. I will be waiting." The Sage opened the door for me.

"How can I communicate with you while I am gone?" I asked The Sage.

"You can't." The Sage's gentle smile reassured me that I would be fine.

"I will see you soon, then," I said, confidently. The Sage nodded his head and closed the door behind me. It didn't seem like any time had passed while I'd been inside the house. I closed my eyes and took a deep breath of the refreshing forest air, as I had many times before. When I opened them again, I looked behind me. The cottage had disappeared.

I held the burlap bag of seeds in my hand and gazed at them for a few minutes. "Only seven days," I said to myself. "Patience."

I thought about what The Sage had said as I walked back towards Concord, towards home.

Seven days had never seemed like such a long time.

DAY 1:

SEEDS OF AWAKENING

    It was early in the morning. I stood up from my bed ecstatically and quickly put on my clothes: a simple, pale red shirt and worn cotton pants. After lacing up my boots, I moved to my desk. My backpack was on the floor; I grabbed it and put the seeds and map from The Sage inside. Opening the door to my house, I felt a soothing wind and a breath of nature's perfume blow over me, increasing my anticipation for the coming days.

    If you were blind and could only rely on your hearing, you might not even realize that Concord exists. Such a quiet town only sates those hungry for comfort, not adventure. Farmers and metalworkers make up most of the landowners in Concord. There is never much of a reason to leave, as the town is entirely self-sufficient. Colorful merchants, cheap entertainers, and weary mercenaries looking for a night's rest are the only interruptions to the town's serenity. Thanks to my hometown, I had experienced far too little of what the world had to offer.

    I pulled the map out of my backpack and took the time to plan my route. It was a fair distance to The Sage's specified location, but across the forest, past the Stronghold of Bastion, and through the hollow seemed to be the fastest way. I had never travelled so deep into the forest, nor to Bastion, and I was uncertain of what I would find along the way. The newness of everything was intoxicating—all I knew of Bastion came from school and a few stories my father had told me as a child. All I had experienced of the world outside Concord was imaginary, built out of details gleaned from other people's stories. But soon, I would get to view the world with my own eyes and form my own opinions.

Before ambling through Concord's peaceful roads, I felt compelled to look upon my own house once more. Though my mother worked tirelessly (less for survival than fulfillment) and was rarely at home during the day, affording me the opportunity to spend most of my time exploring the woods on my own and unquestioned, my hands still quaked and my heart still pumped nervously. However, if I wished to obtain what I sought, I could not make any excuses, no matter how perilous my travels might become.

As I wandered through the forest, I felt that nature was especially inviting on this particular day. The air was permeated by sweet aromas, and the trees stood like pillars, holding up the sky above.

Suddenly, I felt a strong force knock me to the ground.

"What are you doing alone in the woods, huh?" a deep and vicious voice demanded.

My head throbbed with an intense pain that could not allow me to see straight.

"Well, what is it? Are you picking fruit out here? I asked you a question!" the voice snarled before I was struck again.

I was in agonizing pain now.

As I lay on the ground helplessly, I grew angry that these bandits would dare disturb the forest, the place that had always been a quiet place, an escape from civilization.

"Do your ears not work, brat? Do you mind if I look in this bag of yours? If you squirm, I'll knock your brains out of your skull!"

I remained still as one of the two brutes violently stripped me of my pack.

"Some water, a few seeds, and a map. What are you, some sort of gardener? Pathetic!" one of the brigands barked.

I did not say a single word.

"You have no money in here at all, huh? I'm hungry; I guess we'll just have to smash your skull in and have your brains with these little seeds of yours for lunch!" the other one laughed.

It was all over. I began to cry.

"Here it goes!" When you meet your god, tell him I want to taste his blood next!" The brigands laughed hysterically as one of them stomped on my neck to keep my head still. I winced in pain and closed my eyes; the book of my life was about to end abruptly. Just before the brigand's blood-stained club could reach my hand, I heard him let out a blood-curdling screech. As I opened my eyes again, I saw an imposing, scar-covered man looming over the corpse of the brigand who had been filled with life just a few moments before. This new man was bald and had clear, blue, predatory eyes. Dressed only in a cuirass, tough cotton pants, and dusty brown leather boots, I knew he was a mercenary. He beat his chest and began speaking with another man in a joyfully gruff voice.

"Bone Rattle! Criminals should learn that their crimes only pay people like us!"

"Aagh, vigilantes! You scum ruin everything!" the second brigand yelled fearfully, beginning to run away.

"I'm not just some simple vigilante, street rat! I am the apex predator of these lands! I am the Merciless Eagle, vermin! I am Raptor!" the scar-covered man laughed.

The other mercenary, a lanky individual with an almost skeletal frame knocked the brigand to the ground with his battle axe. He wore a long-sleeved linen shirt under a black leather cuirass, as well as a red bandana under a wide-billed black cap. The lanky man, Bone Rattle, drove his black, mud-stained boot into the brigand's neck with so much force that I could hear bones cracking apart. The brigand attempted to gurgle a few words as blood spilled out of his mouth, but Bone Rattle cackled maniacally and ground his boot even harder into the man's neck. Raptor kneeled close to the brigand's face.

"You look so weak and worthless now, like the street rat you are. Did you need to terrorize that poor kid, just to feel even a bit powerful?"

I got up from the forest floor and attempted to recover from the various blows I had just received.

"If you don't cry for me right now, I will lob your head off and put it on my mantle, so you can watch my trysts for the rest of my days helplessly," Raptor said, giggling.

The brigand began to cry and beg for mercy as Raptor began to laugh again. Raptor touched his hand to the brigand's tears and stuck his fingers to his tongue. "The tears of the wicked always taste the sweetest," he said.

I turned away before I could witness Raptor execute the bandit. I heard one final weak moan before he died. I was speechless. Raptor had taken the time to terrorize him and put him through the same mental anguish I had been forced to endure. Although Raptor and Bone Rattle had saved my life, they had also tortured that man in the most revolting way possible, before slaughtering him like livestock.

"Whelp! You're coming with us," Raptor yelled.

"Raptor and Bone Rattle, right? Where are we going?" I asked, nervously. I was still shaken after that ordeal with the bandits, and the gruesome execution I had just witnessed.

"Bastion! I need to collect payment for taking care of those two criminals!" Raptor barked.

I was relieved—they were going exactly where I needed to go.

"You go around without a weapon? You are a crazy little Whelp, aren't you?" Bone Rattle said, cackling.

"I never really thought I needed one; the forest is usually peaceful," I said.

"Nonsense!" Raptor yelled. Raptor stopped walking and grabbed me by the shoulders, violently. "Never go without a weapon! Even if it is a simple little dagger, you never want to be defenseless," he continued in a serious tone. "All of these scars you see covering my body were given to me when I had my sword in my hand. I probably wouldn't have been alive to *get* all these scars if I didn't carry my sword with me all the time!" Raptor said, going back to his carefree tone.

Our trek through the forest resumed. As we walked, I became curious about the many scars Raptor had. "Raptor, where did you get all those scars?"

"From living, Whelp!" he laughed. "I have been a mercenary now for 15 years. I used to be a criminal back when I was your age—stealing from the poor, looting houses, killing innocents for fun. I was probably as evil as the forest is green. I had plenty of warrants out for my arrest, too, but one day, I couldn't run from the law anymore."

I was intrigued. "What happened?" I asked, curious.

"Well, Whelp, I was busy digging through some lady's drawers, looking for jewelry to steal when I heard the door to the house break down. I knew who it was then."

"Who?"

"Frederick, Bastion's finest warrior and general."

I was surprised. Frederick was well known, even in Concord.

"He had come to the house with a whole platoon of soldiers, but he came alone to the room I was in. We fought, my sword against his," Raptor said pensively. "I swung at him first, my sword slicing into his cheek. I expected him to flinch, but he didn't. That Frederick was a tough bastard. He came back with his sword and gave me this pretty little mark right here." Raptor pointed to a large vertical scar on his thigh. "I was dripping blood like a fountain by then; I was a cornered dog. I came at Frederick with everything I had. We traded many more blows before I could feel like I had the advantage. I hit him one good time in the chest, and he fell to his back. His armor cracked where I had connected. It seemed like I had him, but it wasn't over yet."

Bone Rattle and I remained silent, waiting for the conclusion of Raptor's story.

"When Frederick got up, no words could describe the amount of anger I could feel coming from his eyes. I could barely react before I was struck in the face with his shield and knocked to the ground. I still remember feeling a bit of hair come off the moment Frederick plunged his sword dangerously close to my face. I was beaten. Frederick should have killed me that day, but he didn't." Raptor nodded his head, signifying that he had finished telling his tale.

"Why didn't he, you think?" I asked.

"Well, Whelp, I still haven't gotten a straight answer to that one. Frederick ordered his soldiers to chain me up and into the jail I went. I spent about 10 years in that awful place before I was let out. I should have gotten more time. I deserved to rot in that jail for the rest of my life, but, for whatever reason, they only gave me 10 years. It was almost like someone up top had fought for me, so I wouldn't have to spend the rest of my life in that dirty cell. Once I was free, I resolved to leave all the idiotic crime behind me and put my superb swordplay to good use. I wouldn't be here today, had Frederick not spared my life. That Frederick…he still isn't too keen on me, whether he spared my life or not."

The trees around us began to thin out; we were close to the end of the forest. Raptor's story had affected me deeply. A criminal-turned-hero, all because of the mercy of one man. I wondered where Raptor would be now if he had never met Frederick that fateful day.

We were nearing the city now—as we walked down the road, I noticed more carriages and people passing by. It seemed, as we walked along, that I didn't see any two people alike. Very different from Concord.

"Oy! Eagle! Scarred up as ever, aren't you?" yelled a short, foreign-looking man as he waved in our direction. The sword at his side and manner of dress told me he must be a mercenary like Raptor.

"Well met, Momonga! It has been too long! You would have a few more scars yourself if you took on more dangerous mis-

18

sions!"

The man chuckled. "Ay, you just aren't as quick as I, Eagle. But you are no slouch; I hear you have the highest bounty collected among these lands. Word of your exploits turns up at every tavern I've come across since the old days."

Raptor guffawed. "Your quickness is matched only by your frailty, Squirrel. It makes no difference to me either way. A job is a job. The fearful make no money in this business, is all."

The mercenaries shook hands. I could tell that they held great respect for each other by their short, yet spirited, exchange.

"Best of luck, Eagle. I pray you never meet a job fear would save you from. And privateer...what was it again? Bone Bottle? I've not forgotten our night out in Marina. I trust you'll pick up the tab the next time we find ourselves at a bar." The foreign mercenary gripped his scabbard tightly and leered at Bone Rattle before walking away, muttering still. "...damned drunken pirate... no business as mercenary...that overgrown liquor bottle..."

"That's Bone *Rattle* to you!" Bone Rattle yelled out.

"Squirrel's a whole lot more generous than I. If I was left to pick up your enormous bill at every bar and tavern we have been through.... You know that if the bottle didn't kill you, *I* surely would," Raptor snarled.

"Lay off, will you? You remember the story! Our target was leaving the bar, just as the party was getting good! It is no fault of mine that Squirrel's petite constitution can't handle a few drinks! Business comes first, birdie!" Bone Rattle laughed heartily.

We weren't too far from the gates of Bastion when a traveling merchant stopped us.

"You all look like a fine lot of warriors!" the merchant said, his mustache curling while he grinned. Raptor rolled his eyes and groaned.

"You mean, two warriors and a baby, right?" Bone Rattle snickered.

I detested being called a Whelp and a baby, but I held my tongue out of fear of getting roughed up by the mercenaries. The merchant shifted his attention towards me. "Ah! You must need my services! I sell some of the finest arms the world has ever known!"

I could tell by Raptor's unamused expression that he had dealt with a great deal of merchants and salesmen before on his travels. "Well, Whelp, what's it going to be?" Raptor asked impatiently.

"You mean, I should buy a weapon?"

"Well, you were lucky the last time, because I was hunting those street rats; next time, you may not have anyone to defend you but yourself." The merchant proceeded to open the curtain on his cart, which housed a wide variety of different arms: swords, axes, daggers, and other curious, exotic weapons.

"See anything you like?"

I was suspicious of the quality of the merchant's wares. "How do you go about buying these sorts of things?" I asked Raptor and Bone Rattle.

"Something you could actually carry around...maybe that feather over there?" Bone Rattle joked.

"He'll have that short sword over there," Raptor said.

I reached for my wallet but then remembered that I had left it at my house. All I had with me were the seeds, some water, and the map. "But Raptor, I don't have any money with me."

"Don't worry about it. Merchant, bring me the sword."

Raptor put the sword in my hands. The handle was wrapped in sturdy leather, the blade forged out of an illustrious steel. The happy merchant whipped his horse and went on his way. I couldn't understand Raptor's generosity, but I guess there was a heart in even the most hardened people.

"Get ready!" Raptor yelled.

I was startled by his shout. Before I could question what I was to get ready for, I had to dodge out of the way of his sword. A large cloud of dust rose from where I had just stood.

"You are a quick one, aren't you?" Raptor swung once more. I dodged again, but this time, he caught the sleeve of my shirt.

"What did I do to make you angry?" I asked Raptor uneasily.

"Nothing! I bought you a sword; now you have to learn to

use it!" I did not understand how Raptor expected me to learn swordplay without simple instruction first.

"Raptor! I've never fought before! I've never even *held* a sword until now!" I yelled fearfully.

"Whelp! The best fighting comes from instinct! Now stand your ground and fight me!" I dodged another one of Raptor's swings. Before I could recover from dodging the last swing, Raptor quickly swung his blade again and sliced into my arm. Time began to slow. "Your life could very well end today, if you do not best me, here and now! I have no qualms about killing a child!" Raptor exclaimed.

Child. Whelp. Baby. Being called those things was exasperating. Flames built ferociously in my heart. Anger, not reason, began to rule my mind. I had never been so infuriated in all my life. Raptor swung his sword once again, but this time, I did not get out of the way. I parried his swing and quickly swung towards his chest. This time, Raptor was the one who dodged. As he hopped back to avoid being slashed, I tackled him at his legs and knocked him to the ground.

Now I was in control. I used the handle of my sword to viciously pound at Raptor's chest and face. His grunts of pain motivated me to hit him even harder. Raptor let out a powerful roar and threw me off of him. Before he could stand up again, I swung at his chest with all the strength I could muster and once more knocked him to the ground.

I was in a frenzy; my mind abandoned me, as the primal urge to conquer an adversary took over. I saw that my strike had torn his cuirass. *Now* I could end him. I jumped back on top of him and held my sword over his neck.

"Am I a child to you now?" I screamed furiously. "Now I'm going to slaughter you!"

Before I could drive my sword into Raptor's chest, Bone Rattle tackled me and held me to the ground, ignoring my struggling kicks. He slapped me and shook my shoulders. "Have you gone mad, boy? Come back to your senses!" Bone Rattle slapped me once more. I blinked and opened my eyes to the world again. My mind came back to me.

"Good showing, Whelp! You may not know how to use a sword yet, but now you know how to fight for your life," Raptor said proudly.

I felt a stinging pain in my arm, and I remembered that I had been sliced.

"Let's go get these scratches wrapped up in town," Raptor said.

"Well! I would never have imagined I would watch the Merciless Eagle get swatted out of the sky by an ordinary housecat!" Bone Rattle chuckled.

As we walked through Bastion's gates, I wondered if I had always had that primal instinct within me. If Bone Rattle hadn't knocked me off of Raptor, I would have killed a man that day. Maybe the real battle wasn't between Raptor and me, but between my mind and the beast within. There seemed to be a fine line between mastering your instincts and allowing your instincts to master you. Raptor may have been pleased by my performance in our battle, but I was not. I had never lost control over myself like that.

We were coming ever closer to the Stronghold of Bastion, founded by Ogier, a warrior of legendary renown. While he had long since passed, his sword, Caliburn, remains as a testament to the leadership and heroism he displayed in forming the city. Worn, gray walls surrounded the town, protecting it from any sort of attack. Originally the capital of the Unified Lands, it now serves as a small military base, as well as a center of commerce for the surrounded towns, cities, and travelers of all types. We had finally come upon the city's gate.

"State your business in town today, men." The guard before us stood slouched, his face a mask of apathy.

"Just collecting a reward for ending the crime spree of two bandits that had been terrorizing the local areas, Captain," Bone Rattle said.

"Be on your way then, men. Enjoy your time in The Stronghold." The guard moved back to his original position, utilizing his sword as a cane to prop himself up.

"They really do hire the liveliest people for that job, don't they, Raptor?" Bone Rattle said under his breath, giggling. The guard immediately turned to us and scowled; Bone Rattle was a loud whisperer.

As we walked to the infirmary to have our wounds treated, I watched the soldiers running and training in various combat exercises. I could only think of how I would now have a scar of my own, like I assumed all of these men did. If a scar serves as the physical representation of a memory, Raptor must have had more memories than most.

Only a few minutes later, Raptor and I were both sitting in the infirmary, being tended to. "Well, Whelp, we are almost at our destination, but what is yours?" Raptor asked me.

"I was just traveling today," I said, surprised at my words and the spell that The Sage had cast.

"You were not a tough pup when I first met you. You are brittle and weak. But your spirit—it is indomitable. I'll admit, in the beginning of our battle, I gave you the upper hand. But when my sword met your arm, I knew you had changed. That animalistic fury you showed me, I have only seen it once before. The difference between you and that other man is that he could control his fury, and you cannot. Learn how to control that fury, Whelp, and you may be as powerful as that man one day."

When the doctor finished with us, I followed Bone Rattle and Raptor to a wooden desk, behind which sat a rotund, aged man writing diligently and stamping completed warrants. Bone Rattle slammed the head of his axe into the ground and startled the man enough to make him drop his pen. He began to look up angrily but smiled when he realized who had made the noise. "Rattle! You would do well not to make such a racket while I am working!" The man let out a hearty laugh.

"And if I keep at it?" Bone Rattle sneered.

The rotund man pulled an ornate broadsword from under his desk and smiled. Raptor, Bone Rattle, and the man all laughed hysterically; they seemed to be good friends.

"I am coming to collect the reward for 'the arrest or execution of the two bandits who have killed four innocent men and engaged in thievery,'" Raptor said.

"Arrest or execution?"

"Execution."

"Proof?" Raptor pulled out the bandit's shirts and the sack of goods that had been stolen. "You know, you could have arrested a lot of the criminals you have pursued," the man said.

"They call me the Merciless Eagle for a reason," Raptor replied in a serious tone.

"Well, that will be 50 gold pieces for the both of you. Keep up the good work." The rotund man stamped the warrant and put it in a pile with the rest of the completed warrants. The old wooden floorboards creaked quietly as we left.

"You don't eat enough, child," Bone Rattle said, pointing out my rather average constitution.

"You're one to talk, Rattle. I'm surprised you don't spook more people with your skeletal frame," Raptor joked.

"Listen here, Eagle. I've heard no complaints about my body. In fact, the lady I talked to at the bar out in that mining town we passed through last week loved it!" Bone Rattle cackled.

"Ah, yes, the undertaker's daughter? What did she say again...something about never having seen a living corpse before?"

"Gah—you were just jealous," Bone Rattle sneered and turned to me again. "We ought to feed you, at least. It would be in poor taste to let a stray kitten starve to death, after all."

"If you could. I don't want to be a bother," I said tensely.

"What do you think, Rattle? I'd wager a few more coins in debt wouldn't hurt him much at this point. I'm sure you'll have it paid off by the time your hair turns gray," Raptor teased.

"Thank you," I said, still nervous.

"You may want to change that dejected expression, lest I change it for you," he growled.

I winced and cowered slightly. I did not feel at all comfortable with the mercenaries. Their roguish tendencies and ill-mannered humor were polar opposites to the calm and polite dispositions of Concord's citizens.

"Oh, lighten up, will you? You'll need a thicker skin than that to survive in the world. You take us far too seriously." Bone Rattle slapped me on the back powerfully as he cackled goofily.

"As he should," Raptor said before lurching in my direction, causing me to jump back skittishly. His fearsome glare was followed by a small, warm smile that eased my discomfort slightly. "We will head towards the Iron Mill, then. I am famished, too, now that you have brought up the subject of food." Raptor pointed ahead to a building fairly close to the infirmary.

"The Iron Mill? What do they serve there?" I asked curiously as we walked.

"Well, iron, of course! My favorite dish is a warm slab of ore with a refreshing cup of hot metal.... You seem confused, child. You have at least eaten an ingot or two before, haven't you?" Bone Rattle snickered.

I scowled at first, but then I began to laugh and decided to try a little sarcasm. "Yes, Bone Rattle, and they were delicious."

The smell of smoked meat and hearty vegetables floated all around us as we entered the tavern, causing me to salivate uncontrollably. Raptor and Bone Rattle called a waiter as we took a seat at a stone table near the back of the dimly-lit room. Once I had relaxed somewhat, the stone chairs felt surprisingly comfortable. Looking around at the other tables, I saw burly men, soldiers, and a few families enjoying their meals; intermittent, light chatter could be heard all around. My observations came to a halt as our waiter made his way to the table. "Ah, Raptor and Bone Rattle! You'll take a couple of mugs of ale to start, won't you?" The waiter's enthusiasm seemed strange to me.

"Always! Go ahead and tell the kitchen we'll have three beef platters, and water for the boy, if you would." The waiter nodded his head at Raptor's order and quickly went to retrieve our drinks, hastily bringing them to us.

Inspecting the mercenaries, I noticed golden, castle-shaped pins on Raptor's cuirass and Bone Rattle's shirt that I had not seen before. "What are those golden pins for?" I asked them both.

"Every mercenary is processed at a different location across the country. The shape and material of the pin denotes where you were originally processed. The pins are an easy way to identify mercenaries and where they are from. Without them, there would be no order to the warrant system; vigilante justice would run unchecked and corrupt. Squirrel, the foreign man we talked to, was processed in Marina, a harbor town. Their pin is a silver anchor." Raptor subtly pointed to others in the room who also wore pins after explaining them.

"Why would towns pay for mercenaries if they already have guards and night watchmen, though?" I leaned forward, interested to learn more about mercenary life.

"Guards and night watchmen are primarily concerned with petty infractions against the law and with maintaining order among the civilian populations. Mercenaries allow themselves to be bought in order to put their own lives at a higher risk and chase after rats who commit more serious crimes. The more dangerous the criminal or situation, the higher the payment will be for completing the warrant. Rattle and I go after the highest warrants exclusively."

"Are you not worried about the risks involved? Do you not fear death?" I shrank in my seat, not being able to sympathize with his ardor for danger, even if it paid well.

"Whelp, look at that family there." As I glanced at them, I noticed the mother glaring angrily at Raptor before turning back to talk to her family. Before I could speak, Raptor spoke again. "There are many who remember the evils I committed when I was young. People still whisper about my past crimes, all these years later. No matter what I do now, that point in my life has permanently poisoned and stained the rest. I've faced death once before and accepted my fate willingly. I now operate on borrowed time, given to me by the very man who should have killed me. I'd find no pleasure in prolonging my life; courting death is the greatest excitement, never knowing when she will finally let me have her." Raptor drank the rest of his ale in one gulp and let the mug upon the table with a sharp thud.

"...Agh! I was just resting my eyes, is all!" Bone Rattle yelped and jerked back as the sound of Raptor's mug awoke him from his impromptu nap. The waiter arrived with our food and set the hot, appetizing meals on the table. Devouring the platter of delicious food left me full and in a euphoric daze.

"Take this and keep the rest. Good work as always." Raptor pulled two gold pieces from his pocket and gave them to the waiter.

"Thank you!" the waiter exclaimed happily, leaving the table hastily.

"Two gold pieces!" I said, astounded at the enormous tip he had left the waiter. "Our meals, including drinks, must have been 30 silver coins at the most!"

"Hot meals and great service are what allow me to go out and make my income. If you have the coin, it is worth letting go of a little extra to the best workers. Hell, bring the king in here, and I'd gamble half of my store of gold we would still receive better service," Raptor sneered while he finished his meal.

Raptor's definition of "a little extra" certainly does not match my own, I thought.

"Speak for yourself, birdie," Bone Rattle said, belching loudly enough to anger the family sitting next to us. "I haven't the same sweet, endearing personality that you do. I couldn't make a bet like that against the king," he finished sarcastically, cleaning his teeth with a small bone, giggling as always.

"All right, we've kept you alive and taught you how to not be so feeble. Your debt will be waived if you quit following us around like a lost kitten. I haven't the temperament to take care of pets," Raptor growled. He wanted to seem tough and aloof, but my fear of him had dwindled significantly since we first met. As we exited the tavern, I looked at the horizon and sighed; the first day of many was almost complete.

"Whelp, before we part ways, I have something for you," Raptor said, bringing me out of my thoughts for a moment. "Bone Rattle and I are the greatest mercenaries around, but we wouldn't have caught those vermin, had they not stopped to torment you. Go ahead and take these 10 gold pieces—five from Rattle and five from me." Raptor put the gold pieces in a small sack and handed them to me.

"I can't accept this," I said sternly.

"Don't be a stubborn brat and take it," he growled.

"I did nothing to deserve this, Raptor. I appreciate the gesture, but I can't."

"Raptor sighed and put the gold pieces in his bag.

Looking into the sky, I could see the sun begin to fall, its rays slowly releasing their grip from the landscape.

"Thank you for everything, Raptor." A strange sense of candid fraternity came over me, looking into Raptor's eyes.

"Ah, yes—I don't recall a second mercenary being there to save your life," Bone Rattle quipped.

"…and Bone Rattle," I said, chuckling.

"Well, Whelp—" Before Raptor could finish his sentence, I cut him off.

"Don't call me Whelp," I told him assertively.

"So, you finally built up the courage to tell me to stop, huh? There is some hope for you yet," Raptor laughed. Then, his face changed once again to his customary scowl. "The Eagle has shown you mercy once. Take this gold or you won't be so lucky the next time we cross swords," he warned me.

I nodded my head and reluctantly accepted his charity. "This is where we part ways," I said.

Raptor stared me down for a few seconds, his fearsome, cerulean eyes acutely scrutinizing me. "I can see it in your eyes, kid—you really are after something, aren't you? Something to make you feel alive? That's what everyone wants. For me, I've wanted to feel alive all my life. The only times I do are in battle, when I'm bloodied and close to death. In those moments, fighting for my life, I feel truly alive. Between those moments, I'd be better off dead. I'd prefer my life to be like the brilliant strike of lightning, rather than the long, untroubled burning of a candle. Lightning, while fleeting, is exciting. It burns gloriously and leaves all who see it amazed, stupefied even. I look at a candle for the same fleeting moment after lighting it, and that is it. No wonder, no exhilaration. It may burn for an eternity, but what does it matter? Go out there and live like lightning, kid." Raptor seemed to have reflected deeply while he spoke.

I shook hands with the two brutish, yet gallant, mercenaries and with that, my adventures with them had ended. For now, at least.

I walked down the cobbled road to the hollow. *Live like lightning.* Those words echoed in my head like a thunderclap. The setting sun allowed the shadows of the surrounding trees and buildings to dance once more before the night arrived. As I walked through the hollow, I could see the animals preparing to go back to their homes. I, too, had to go back to my home, but only after planting the seeds.

A small patch of barren soil rested just past the hollow's exit. It seemed as if there had been no one there in years. I reached into my sack and grabbed the seeds, as well as the water I had brought from my house. I dug a small hole into the patch of fertile soil and put the seeds there. After covering the seeds with the soil, I patted it down and poured a generous amount of water over the seeds. It only took a few moments for the seeds to sprout and grow. The four sprouts grew and wrapped into one another to form one singular sapling.

Six more days, I thought to myself. *Six more days, and I'll have all the time in the world.*

Today, I not only planted the seeds of the tree but the seeds of my adventure, as well.

DAY 2:

KNOWLEDGE PERSONIFIED

      Crossing the forest to Bastion's giant gates the following day left me weary, yet hopeful about the day ahead. Unlike the day before, this day's trip had remained peaceful. My grip around the handle of my sword tightened, as I thought of my encounter with the bandits. Although Concord never had a problem with crime, I didn't like realizing that I would never have been able to protect my mother and myself, if anything were to happen to us. I was no longer defenseless, and while I was no warrior like the mercenaries that had gifted me the blade, I knew that I could at least fight to defend my mother and myself if our lives were ever thrust into jeopardy.

      My boots made tapping noises against the cobblestone streets as I walked through town. I couldn't help but look at each passerby and wonder about his or her story. Raptor's words echoed in my head once again: "No wonder, no exhilaration. It may burn for an eternity, but what does it matter?" Although I still couldn't understand the mercenaries' way of life, I knew Raptor had a point. The conviction he held about his life made me think hard, but I knew I still wanted to live like the candle and not the lightning. *Maybe I could live like both*, I thought. Between the two of them, Raptor and Bone Rattle contained enough stories to fill a library, but they were extraordinary examples. Most people do the same things every day, living only one story all their lives.

The thought of Raptor and Bone Rattle filling a library made me think: a visit to the library could help make more sense of The Sage and his many secrets.

Looking at the library's intricate pillars and marbled appearance a few minutes later, I attempted to piece together what I already knew about The Sage in my head. The local myths and legends painted The Sage as a timeworn soul whose wisdom was as vast as his hair was white, but I knew this was not the case. The Sage, while incredibly wise, did not seem to be as old as the legends had made him out to be.

The library was small but contained a fair number of shelves. I knew it would take me a long time to find what I wanted on my own, so I made my way to the librarian at the front desk. "How may I help you?" she inquired in a drab tone.

"I'm looking for books about The Sage; could you help me find them?" I asked.

"Ah, The Sage, you say? Many great works of fiction have spawned from that myth." The librarian seemed to be an avid reader, but I suppose that was not surprising.

"Do you have anything about the myth itself, specifically?" I asked, hoping that she could show me a book of facts, not fiction.

"Right this way."

The librarian led me towards a shelf that sat in the far corner of the library. "This shelf contains all of our books about the myths and legends of the land. Let me look closely here.... Ah, and here is our section specifically on The Sage." The librarian grabbed a worn, leather-bound tome from the shelf. "This book contains many myths, but it does have a great deal about The

Sage. I hope this will help." The librarian handed me the tome and slowly walked back to her desk.

The ragged leather created a cracking noise as I opened the book, my mind eagerly searching for more about the enigmatic figure who had devised this journey. I enjoyed reading, but no book had ever truly consumed me. I had always been thirsty to *live* stories, not to read them.

"That is quite an old book for such a young man to be reading."

A soft, yet commanding voice gently ended my meditation and brought me back to the task at hand. The origin of the voice was a man clothed in a pale red robe. His well-kempt hair was a deep mahogany, and there was a surprisingly youthful face hidden behind his neatly-trimmed beard. He was the personification of rugged sophistication.

"Does that seem strange to you?" I asked. I could feel the man's emerald eyes analyzing me from behind his rounded spectacles; they reminded me of eyes I had seen before.

"I have only ever known one person your age to delve this deeply into the library's books." The man smiled; a wave of nostalgia noticeably softened his shrewd demeanor. "Bertrand," he stated, reaching his hand out to shake. Then, "The Sage?"

His meticulous observation surprised me. I could feel The Sage's magic tightening around my lips. "I was just reading about him for fun." Bertrand looked as if he knew I had ulterior motives for researching The Sage.

"No one reads tomes like that for fun. I haven't even read this one...not for fun, at least," Bertrand smirked.

"I was just curious about the myth is all," I said, The Sage's magic speaking for me.

"Come, friend. Let us take a walk...unless you believe you could learn more out of that leather-bound paperweight than you could from me."

I was skeptical at first, but I surmised that Bertrand would have more information to offer me than some old book.

As we walked out of the library, I could feel the warm summer air caressing my skin and cool zephyrs from different lands waltzing between the buildings and through the streets. The scent of flowers was prominent in Bastion today. Merchants lined up on the street selling various types of food and wares. It did not take long for Bertrand to find the source of the floral aroma in the air—one merchant's cart was filled with a rainbow of different flowers; every color was represented.

"Excuse me for a moment," Bertrand said.

While Bertrand looked at the different flowers on the merchant's cart, I decided to quickly grab something to eat. When I came back to the flower cart, Bertrand was curiously absent. I turned in all directions, attempting to find his pale red robe in the crowd of bodies. After a few minutes, I finally found him.

"I picked this flower out just for you. Do you know what it is? It is an exotic rarity, like yourself." The beautiful woman to whom Bertrand was talking giggled and smiled as he continued to allure her with his words. "I am blessed that the gods would give such a flower as beautiful as you the chance to be human. Take this fire lily from me, and with it, my heart." Bertrand's every move—his subtle touches, his sensual winks, every word he spoke—seemed to flow effortlessly as the woman fell deeper and deeper in love with him. "Alas, my sweet fire lily, I must depart. I do not know when I will return. The flower you hold in your hands is my heart; I will let you keep it while I am gone. A man cannot live without his heart forever, though. I am sure you will keep it safe for me, yes?" Bertrand embraced the woman and kissed her passionately, his performance complete.

I could not believe what I had seen. Bertrand had turned a flower into a potential bride, in the same amount of time it had taken me to eat a chicken kebab.

"Bertrand!" I exclaimed.

"Yes, friend? Are you ready to go for our walk?" Bertrand asked, resuming his sapient behavior.

"You…how did you do that?" I asked him.

"Do what?"

"Oh, you know. *That!*" It was hard to tell whether he was

joking or really didn't know what I meant.

"We will go down this road here; it tends to be peaceful," Bertrand said, blatantly ignoring my questions. I wanted to press the point one more time but I didn't bother. Bertrand seemed able to shift between two roles instantly—sage one second, seducer the next.

We walked to a quaint little road bordered by trees that seemed to bow over travelers, providing a refreshing shade. "Who was the one other person my age that you met in the library reading those ancient tomes?" I asked eventually.

"I didn't meet that person, friend. I was that person. When I was around your age, I was obsessed with the acquisition of knowledge. In school, I was always the person to receive the highest grades. When I couldn't learn any more from books, I began to learn from the people around me, but when the people around me couldn't teach me anymore, I became frustrated. My teachers became frustrated, as well, as they couldn't possibly match their finest pupil. I had become their equal and then surpassed them." Bertrand seemed to become more dejected as he spoke.

"That is quite a gift you have, Bertrand, your intelligence," I said, attempting to raise his spirits, but I could sense that it was of no use.

"A gift for the world, maybe, not for me. At first it was great, having all these adults shower me with attention because of my wits. After a while, though, people tend to despise someone more intelligent than they," Bertrand sighed. I remained silent.

The song of birds filled the trees as we walked farther down the road. The road Bertrand was leading me down, and the sound of the birds, reminded me of walks I took with my father when I was younger. "If we could understand the songs birds sing, we would know all of what happens across the land," he used to say. "Bards spend their lives searching for inspiration, traveling the world to make their songs. Birds fly all over us and see so much more than we can. It is no wonder they are always singing."

If that were so, maybe the birds were still singing about my father and me.

After a fair amount of walking, we reached a small wooden hut that seemed to have been built years ago. "I sat in the library in the very spot you did, reading about The Sage." Bertrand's face lit up again. "You know the general myth, yes? The Sage was an ordinary man, like you or me. The myths paint him to be an omnipotent figure that suddenly graced the world with his brilliance, but that is not the case. The Sage, whoever he was, worked incessantly to possess the sort of knowledge he supposedly had. The general myths tend to forget this part of the story. Tales from tomes older than the one you had today speak of a plant that only bears one fruit every 500 years. Any person lucky enough to stumble upon this curious fruit was granted complete omniscience. While none of the earlier versions of the myth speak of such a plant, they do always talk about The Sage's sudden appearance into the world." Bertrand's analysis of The Sage's myth was already more detailed than what I had read.

"So, you mean that…"

Before I could finish my thought, Bertrand continued speaking. "The Sage must have come across that very fruit in his travels and become instantly wise." I thought about everything that I had heard Bertrand say. I realized there was only one question I could ask Bertrand that would really matter. I shifted my gaze towards the wooden hut where we had stopped; its image was a reminder of the humble hut where I had stopped two days ago.

"Is The Sage still alive?" I asked Bertrand nervously. Bertrand's face turned puzzled; he looked as if he thought my question was frivolous.

"Of course not. While I believe The Sage was a lot more than just a legend, he would have to have been dead for centuries now."

I attempted not to look unbelieving, but I knew The Sage was alive; I had met him. We continued to walk down the road, the shade growing darker, the air around us becoming cooler. "Bertrand, why did you wish to learn so much about The Sage in the first place?" Bertrand glanced towards me and gave a small smile.

"My only love has been the acquisition of knowledge. The Sage is the embodiment of who I wish to be." He began to mumble to himself. "That fruit...if I could only find that fruit..." I understood him now. To Bertrand, The Sage wasn't just some legend; he was a goal to be achieved. Even his eyes were like The Sage's, except that while Bertrand's eyes analyzed, The Sage's eyes simply knew. The difference, though subtle, was crucial. There was a certain kind of pain I could see in Bertrand, though. I wondered if he would find solace from his ongoing quest for knowledge.

The tree branches shook in the wind, giving the impression that they were saying goodbye. The road had taken us out towards the eastern gate of the city. The hollow was not too far off. I started to ask Bertrand another question, but a pair of eyes just ahead silenced me. I had never seen eyes as spectacular as hers. The radiance they projected warmed my soul in a way I had never felt before. My gaze locked on hers; even the gods could not have broken me away from her spellbinding stare. An eternity passed between us before I was knocked out of my stupor by Bertrand asking what had caught my eye.

"Huh?" I asked, my brain still muddled by her fascinating form.

"I don't think I see what you are seeing, friend."

It was not surprising—she was quite a modest-looking girl, overall, but that made her more beautiful to me. She was a treasure that only I could see. I wanted to walk towards her, but I felt paralyzed. With a seductive smirk, she turned away from me.

Her eyes had given me a taste of the immortality that I so intensely desired.

"Take this and go talk to her." Bertrand had picked a wildflower and put it in my hand.

"I don't know if I can do that," I said, nervously.

"How did you get that wound?" he asked, pointing to my arm.

"I got in a fight with a mercenary," I told him, nonchalantly.

"Yes? So you mean to tell me that you can bring a sword into battle, but you can't bring a flower to a cute little girl? Well," he continued a moment later. "I think I may have reconsidered. She is rather beautiful, isn't she?"

I gasped. I had already seen what Bertrand was capable of; I could not allow him to work his terrible talents on this girl! I mustered what courage I had and walked closer to her.

"I couldn't help but notice you. Are you from around here?" I asked when I reached her. She turned to me but remained silent. "I picked this for you." I waited as her expression, cold and expressionless, began to paralyze me again. After a few moments, the girl let out a sweet little giggle that suffocated my heart.

"Thanks," she said curtly, grabbing the flower out of my hand. "What's your name?" I asked her as she began to walk away. I expected a response, but my question was left unanswered. Right before she walked into a local pub, she turned to me and grinned. I was confounded; I could not help but want to learn more about this stony-eyed curiosity.

"How did it go?" Bertrand asked me when I returned.

"I guess she likes me," I told him uncertainly.

"Friend, you should know whether a girl likes you from the first few moments of interaction. Her eyes will grow wide, to see more of you. Her body's movements will make it appear to be dancing with you. Her voice will soften and sweeten, like a song, requesting you to love and protect her. You did not notice any of these things?"

"Well...she did say thank you for the flower."

"A polite little faerie you've fallen in love with, it seems," Bertrand concluded dryly. It didn't help.

I wondered if I would see the girl again. Bastion was a small city, but a city nonetheless. *The sun is beginning to set*, I thought to myself. "It must feel good to be so naturally talented with women," I remarked. Bertrand laughed. "Why do you laugh?"

"You assume I was always so good because I make it look effortless, but that is not the case. Like I said, when I couldn't learn from books, I learned from others. When I was younger, I would watch men who had the most luck with ladies on my way to classes: their subtle movements, their words, their expressions. Eventually, I just learned to imitate what they were doing right and worked to forget my bad habits."

"I don't think I could ever be as good as you," I said, honestly.

Grinning, Bertrand replied, "Friend, natural talent, while helpful, is ultimately meaningless. The only natural talent I have ever had was a strong propensity to learn. All other skills I have accumulated over the course of my life have been through study and patience." Bertrand spoke quite sincerely on this topic.

"Thank you for everything you have taught me. I must be on my way."

"Where are you going, anyway?" Bertrand inquired as he shook my hand goodbye.

"Home." The magic had bound my lips yet again.

"Ah, well. I hope you won't remain a stranger! If you ever wish to help me conduct research, or even share a drink, my home is right here." I felt proud to have become a friend to such an interesting and intelligent person. Before I could turn my back and walk towards the hollow, Bertrand stopped me. "You like music, yes?"

"I do enjoy listening to the bards from time to time."

"You can think of every piece of knowledge you come across as an instrument. Your mind acts as the composer. Your thoughts are like songs, and with every new instrument, each song will become more sonorous and melodic than the last. Learn as much as you can, friend, and your life will become a symphony." Bertrand gave me a final smile and entered his house.

As I walked through the hollow again, I thought of everything I had learned on my journey so far. It was only the second day of this adventure, but I had learned more about myself and the world over the course of these two days than I had ever learned before. I took what Bertrand had said to heart. There was much to be learned from the world around me, if I took the time. I thought back to what my father had said about the birds those years ago, and I smiled.

The sapling's leaves fluttered gently as I approached. I took the water from my backpack and poured a generous amount over the plant. The sapling quickly grew again, sprouting more branches and becoming taller than I. I looked up and remembered the seeds that I had planted only the day before. Each day was unimaginable; each day brought with it new people, new adventures.

Turning my back to the tree, I felt a wave of excitement rush over me.

"Five days from now, my adventures will never end."

DAY 3:

BELLADONNA

Relying only on what Raptor had taught me about courage in the midst of battle would be useless if I did not supplement with auxiliary knowledge—courage without knowledge would lead to impetuous action, but knowledge without courage would lead to cowardly observation.

To that end, I borrowed a book on swordplay from the library and decided to use what time I had before visiting the tree to work on my swordsmanship. I knew Raptor would want a rematch if we crossed paths once again.

The forest's calming interior would function as my classroom for today's training session. I opened the book; its yellowed pages were filled with different stances, strikes, blocks, and parries. The sword's leather-bound handle reminded me of the leather-bound tome I had held in my hands yesterday. Learning more about The Sage had only created more questions.

I practiced relentlessly for hours that day, working on my

stance as well as a variety of swings and lunges. I could feel my skills sharpening with each strike. I thought back to the fight with Raptor after I concluded my training. I could tell now that he'd been holding back more than I had initially realized. I vowed to myself that I would eventually become an even match for the battle-hardened mercenary.

As I sat in the shade, recovering from my training, my senses were aroused by a perfume that seemed to pervade the forest. I stood up and scanned the area, then walked through the trees until I reached another clearing. The dull noise of a tree being struck became louder the further I walked. *Could someone else be training out here today?* I thought to myself, perplexed. I didn't believe my eyes when I finally reached the origin of both the scent and the sound.

She had a sword like my own, but she carried hers with much more precision and skill. Each strike was coordinated to such a degree that the tree began to wobble more with each slash; it would not be long before it toppled to the ground. Proving me right, she gave one final swing, and the tree whistled through the air as it fell to the ground. As she turned, I noticed that she was wearing a wildflower in her hair. Time stopped as my eyes met their match once more; the spider had trapped its prey yet again.

"Do you remember me?" I asked her, more calmly than I expected. She remained quiet, but her sword let out a metallic roar as she freed it from its scabbard.

"Draw your blade," she commanded.

I thought of what Bertrand had asked me the day before: "So you mean to tell me you can bring a sword into battle, but you can't bring a flower to a cute little girl?" He would surely be surprised to see me doing the former against that same cute girl to whom I had brought a flower only the day before.

I dodged out of the way of her first swing and drew my sword, recovering from her attack. I barely blocked her second strike, jumping away to come up with a battle plan. While she wasn't as strong as Raptor, her strikes and thrusts were fast and precise; it would be difficult to face her onslaught head-on. I would have to vary my attack with feints and parry what blows I could not dodge. I thrust my blade towards her but met air.

Within an instant, I felt her blade cut gently across my side. *Only a scratch*, I thought, flinching from the sting.

I wasted precious moments, chiding myself for ending up in this situation. *If I had just ignored her yesterday.... Then again, she might have killed me just now if I had never given her that flower...*

Reflection would not help me now. Like a snared insect, I would have to play her perilous game to its conclusion.

Swinging my blade against hers, I could feel her grip loosening slightly before she clenched the handle of her sword once more.

Almost dropped it! If I could overpower her...

I swung clumsily, feeling my stamina begin to lag. As she dodged out of the way, I couldn't help but peer into her eyes yet again. I could sense a daunting complexity emanating from behind them. With a grin, she made it clear that she was aware of my study.

Breathing heavily and deeply, I maneuvered around her slowly, sidestepping her pokes and jabs, rather than recklessly wasting my strikes. I saw an irritated desperation creep up in her. Her agility and obvious talent slowly turned to a rash ruthlessness, one upon which I would be able to capitalize, once her frustrations had reached their peak.

"What's your name?" I asked, hoping to use her sagging energy to my advantage.

"Too tired to fight anymore?" she challenged, angrily changing the subject.

"Maybe you should try training with moving targets, rather than something stationary like that tree, and then you'd be able to hit me!" I yelled condescendingly.

A scarlet glow bubbled across her face as she boiled with rage.

"You!" she fumed.

Her fury led to a hasty blow that I was able to parry with ease. Utilizing all of my strength, I swung viciously, knocking her sword skyward. She yelled indignantly; her sword fell in the grass, far away from her reach. Before she could scramble to reclaim it, I dropped my sword and tackled her to the ground.

"Well?" I asked, breathing heavily.

Admitting defeat, she told me, "Belladonna. But you can call me Bella."

"How long have you been practicing your swordsmanship?" I asked her, sitting up and helping her do the same.

"Once or twice," she answered snidely. "And you?"

"Once or twice." I grinned sarcastically.

"What next then, Traveler?"

Surprised, I asked, "You mean to go with me?"

"Well, if you aren't occupied. You did give me a flower, after all." Bella looked straight into my eyes, and I could feel it again—that immortality. I would certainly go somewhere—anywhere—with her.

As we walked through the forest, I began to tell her stories of the previous days. "I was in this very spot when the bandits attacked me. Two mercenaries saved my life that day. You know, they aren't too bad once you get to know them....

"Without a little push, I might never have talked to you, but one of my friends insisted....

"There are so many different people out there, with vastly different stories....

"Bella, what sorts of adventures have you been on?" I asked, turning to her. She looked at me and smiled a smile that both relaxed me and stoked the flames of my attraction.

"I don't reveal myself so easily, Traveler," she giggled. I was completely intoxicated by her form. Her beautiful hazel eyes seemed to see something within me that I could not even see within myself. Every moment I could make her smile became a taste of eternity. "I will say this, though," she continued, a tinge of anger behind her playful tone. "You won't be so lucky the next time our swords meet."

"We'll see." I smiled, though I could tell that she was not the one to be bested often.

The edge of the forest had come sooner than I had expected. We walked down the well-traveled road to make our way towards Bastion. The weather was agreeable, and each cool breeze was enough to bring on a pleasant shiver. Merchants, soldiers, mercenaries, and common folk were all common sights; it was never unusual to see a mix of people traveling on this road. Our walk remained quiet and relaxed.

"I'm not from around here; where is your favorite place to be?" Bella asked me.

"I'll just take you there." The Sage had said that I was the only person whose eyes could see the tree; its birthplace really had become my favorite spot, and I did need to tend to it.

"You won't tell me?"

"I don't reveal myself so easily." I glanced over at her and smiled.

"You know, your sense of humor might put a red mark on your face very soon."

I told Bella about the different parts of the city as we continued towards the hollow. I liked the idea that she thought of me as a Bastion native; I couldn't help but encourage her in that line of thinking.

Soldiers were exercising outside today, and as we walked through, we saw them all begin to run to the city's center.

"Do they always run this way?"

I shrugged. "They do run every day, but not usually here."

As we got closer to the middle of the action, we realized that we had inadvertently joined a celebration of some sort. It was unlike any I had ever seen. Groups of dancers, all clothed in colorful, exuberant dresses and robes paraded around the streets, energizing all who beheld their gambols. Merchants went through the crowds selling various dishes and sweets, some that I had never seen before. Before long, the smell of all the foods and desserts had caused me to salivate like a starved dog.

"Traveler, could we stay for a little bit? I'm curious about what is going on."

"I don't see why we have to rush," I told her happily.

I didn't know what all this was about, but in every direction was an inexplicable joy which could only be contained by a festival of this magnitude. The smells of chilis, coriander, curry, meat, and a whole regiment of other hunger-inducing odors guided my steps more than anything else.

"Have you ever been to anything like this?" I asked Bella.

"No." Bella was obviously enthralled, but even so, she continued with, "We don't have to stay long."

"Let's see what all this bustle is for," I said, smiling. I grabbed her hand, but she snatched it back quickly.

"I don't need your help getting from place to place, Traveler," she said coldly.

I frowned slightly, but I didn't say anything.

At the town square stood a man dressed in a brilliant suit of armor. His hair was almost as gray as the surrounding buildings. As we got closer to the podium, I could see a prominent scar on his cheek. I remembered Raptor's story about Frederick; I knew then that I was looking at Bastion's finest solder.

"The Stronghold has been home to me for as long as I can remember," he was saying to the crowd. "Early on, I saw what a beautiful city this is, and I revered its defenders. As such, I always dreamed of becoming a soldier. There was nothing more exciting to me than giving my life to something greater than myself. When I joined the military, I made the decision that the lives of my fellow countrymen were greater than my own. As you grow older though, you begin to truly realize what sort of responsibility that is. Responsibility—that is the lifeblood of any enterprise."

"Who is that?" Bella asked, stirred by Frederick's speech.

"Frederick. He has been a part of Bastion's military for years now." It felt unreal to see Raptor's strongest adversary in the flesh.

"Do you see that scar on his cheek?" Bella nodded her head. "I met the man who left that scar," I said, pretending to be casual.

"Really?" Bella rolled her eyes. "I don't believe it."

"Maybe you'll meet him one day; people around here call him the Merciless Eagle."

"...I have had friends, brothers, die in my arms," Frederick was saying now. "I am blessed to have made it this far, but I want everyone to take the time to honor those who were not as lucky. Their sacrifice is the reason this celebration could have occurred. Quite a surprise, I did not expect this sort of birthday this year...."

"This codger sure can talk.... To talk and talk and talk, ad nauseum...." Bella gritted her teeth impatiently.

"We'll give it a few more minutes, and if he isn't done, we'll go about our business."

"As you wish." Bella gritted her teeth with dissatisfaction.

I watched the sundial tick by as Frederick continued to speak, and speak, and speak...an hour had almost gone by the time I looked back at the man speaking.

"...So, gratefully, I stand before you, honored that this city would take the time to venerate me in such a fantastic way. Thank you all for your time and enjoy the rest of the festivities set before us today."

"I'm surprised we didn't all run out of air to breathe. I was beginning to get worried," Bella joked next to me.

"Well, you heard the man; let's—"

Before I could finish, dancers grabbed out hands and began to spin and pull us around the celebration. I was not a particularly good dancer, but Bella did not seem to care. The music and dancers created a tempest of vibrant color. The monochromatic gray of Bastion's architecture was the perfect backdrop for all the colors and cuisines and entertainments and indescribable euphoria that permeated the entire city. As we danced and swayed to the music, I closed my eyes and smiled.

"Traveler, what drew you to me?" Bella asked me suddenly. I heard a defensive tone in her voice.

"I'm not sure. Why were you so short the first time we talked?"

"I've never been interested in making friends. Besides, it was funny to see your reaction. I could tell you hadn't talked to many girls." She giggled mischievously.

I blushed. "Well—"

"It was certainly endearing. In a strange way."

I noticed now how different she looked from everyone else. It was more than just her physicality—I felt like some special piece of her remained invisible to everyone but me. I couldn't quite discern it now, but it was there.

As the celebration continued, Bella and I worked to taste food from every cart—a difficult process, as her taste in food was the complete opposite of mine.

"Try these rice cakes, Bella, they are from some far-off land. We won't see these again any time soon." As I savored each bite of the delicious morsel, Bella promptly spit what little bit of precious rice cake she had in her mouth onto the ground.

"Too soft."

I just looked at Bella and shook my head, I couldn't help but laugh. After a few seconds, she couldn't stop herself from laughing, either.

We traveled to another cart that was covered in a strange green and velvety cloth. My stomach turned at the scent coming from the pans lining the interior of the cart.

"Mmmm, finally! Something appetizing!" Bella cheered.

"You aren't talking about this cart, are you?" I gagged at the rotten odor.

"Oh, you haven't tried it yet."

Looking around, I noticed that this cart was strangely empty of customers—not surprising, as it gave off the aura of a wastebasket on a hot day.

"We'll have two, please," Bella said to the owner of the cart. Within a minute, we were handed two wrapped orders. "Now go ahead and try it; I'm sure you will love it!"

"Okay..." Bella was optimistic; I was not.

I put a bite of the smelly food into my mouth and bit down reluctantly. As soon as I felt its texture and tasted what it was like, I moved far away from the cart, so as not to offend the merchant inside and retched all over the ground.

"You just can't appreciate good food," Bella said as she devoured the rest of her strange, unpalatable dish.

"Food? I wouldn't dare call whatever that was food," I

laughed once I'd recovered from the ordeal.

Bella laughed and then quickly returned to her usual seriousness and began pulling me through the crowd.

Time did not exist within this wonderful bubble of happiness, but external factors served as a reminder that we would have to work our way out of the city soon and towards the tree. The sky's color shifted from a deep cerulean to an eye-catching violet. As the sun began its daily descent, its final rays of light caused the clouds to turn a brilliant golden shade that made the day feel like a treasure in and of itself.

"Hey," Bella said firmly.

"Yes?"

"I've had fun today."

As we locked eyes, I noticed every intricate detail that made her beautiful to me. The city faded away; she was all that mattered. Her hair glowed luminously in the light, revealing an almost golden color, like the clouds that slowly began to fade with the sunset. My eyes slowly moved to her smile, one so contagious I could not help but smile as well. I grabbed her hand and brought her closer to me, her chest now resting against mine.

"Traveler—"

Before she could finish her thought, my lips met hers. She grabbed me forcefully at first, but after a few seconds, I could feel her grip loosen. She slowly moved her hand to my chest as I grabbed her by the waist. We continued kissing; each moment that passed made it more difficult to stop.

"Let's go, Bella," I said as I pulled away from her.

"Will you finally tell me where you are taking me?"

"You'll see."

We walked to the outskirts of the city, the setting sun gently easing us toward the birthplace of the tree. Throughout our whole day together, the one thing I had learned for sure about Bella was how little I had actually learned about her. Her interests, passions, and past all remained an elusive mystery. To that end, I looked over at her and asked, "Bella, where do you come from?"

I could tell that she was hesitant to answer my question.

"I come from many places. Like you, I travel. I live my life as an errant leaf, blown across the land. There is no one place I call home." Bella looked as if she was holding back, but I continued to ask her questions.

"And of your family?"

Bella looked down and sucked wind through her teeth, making a dull, high-pitched whistle.

"My family? I barely remember people I could call my family. My parents were petty thieves and lived in poverty. The money they stole all went to the cheapest spirits they could find. I assume that, one fateful day, they were simply too drunk to remember me—they left me in a filthy alley, and that is where I remained, weak and defenseless."

A deep sorrow for this girl rose in my gut. She continued to speak solemnly.

"I was ignored by all of the people that walked by. None of them could spare even a morsel for me. My body was withering by the day. When I had lost all hope, I heard a harsh cackle from someone which worked to revive my spirits a bit. He looked like Death, but oddly, he was the only one who'd deemed my life worth living. His generosity.... I wonder where he is today."

I could see that her heart was inured to the cruel indifference of the world. Bella did not travel out of desire, but necessity. She was a wanderer in search of catharsis; to find proof of love within the vast void of apathy that consumed the world.

"What are you after in this life?" Bella stopped and questioned me.

"Time, I suppose," I answered her. "And you?"

"Power."

I looked at her despondently and silently.

The hollow was eerily quiet as we approached. The sun's final beams of light pointed us toward the birthplace of the tree.

"Why is this your favorite place to go?"

I could feel the magic begin to tighten around my lips. "I like it because it is quiet; it is a perfect place to relax and think."

Bella looked at me as if evaluating my intentions. Unbeknownst to her, we now stood underneath the tree, its sturdy branches moving over us like a friend inclining his head to listen more deeply to the conversation.

"You value solitude. The silence is refreshing, yes? Too much silence quickly turns into a curse, though. Everywhere I go, I am alone, but I am always accompanied by silence. I hate it, but it was necessary to become comfortable with the silence. I decided to make my only companion my friend, instead of my enemy. I resented all those people who did not need to become accustomed to it, to the silence. I have seen more than most can ever imagine, but it has all been in the company of silence, until today. You…you have shown me that silence need not be my only friend. Traveler…thank you." Bella's embrace warmed my entire body. As I wrapped my arms around her, I could see tears begin to roll down her face. I held her close as she continued to weep.

"Ugh, I hate for anyone to see me like this!" she whimpered angrily. Her body curled away from mine, moving away towards the object only I could see.

As Bella's tears hit the ground, the tree began to grow once more, spreading its branches across the sky. Its height now easily surpassed my own. We laid down next to the tree; I continued to hold Bella in my arms as my eyes shifted towards the sky. It was a weird pain, watching her cry. If I could have done anything to help her, I would have, but there was nothing to do, other than hold her close. Her tears slowly subsided, and I could feel her breaths begin to slow. Without a word, she fell asleep curled up next to me, one of her hands resting gently on my chest.

I did not know how to describe the warmth permeating my spirit as I pulled Bella closer to me and turned my thoughts to The Sage. "I wonder if you know about this feeling, Sage," I murmured, closing my eyes to join Bella in a peaceful slumber.

DAY 4:

THE CHASE

I woke up early in the morning and, to my surprise, Bella had disappeared without notice. Walking back home, I thought about our experience at the festival and all of Bella's interesting peculiarities. Silently skulking though our small, creaky house, I finally reached my bed without disturbing my mother. In it, I fell asleep once more, resting my body and mind for another day.

Some time later, I got up and left the house again, planning on making my way through the woods and to the hollow early. I enjoyed the silence and invigorating air that greeted me. Bella's feeling about silence was the polar opposite of my own. To me, noise was ever present, and any pleasant effects it had to offer began to spoil from the slightest bit of over-exposure. But silence was a different fruit all together. Its scarcity made it precious; every moment devoid of sound was to be savored and remembered. Silence was akin to a hidden treasure, and only the most adept of listeners could appreciate its soothing nature. After listening to Bella's story, however, I came to the realization that silence could not be enjoyed without the existence of noise. For someone constantly surrounded by silence, noise becomes the object of desire.

"You are a faerie, Bella, but I am beginning to believe you are more than just that," I murmured. My thoughts shifted to the tree, and with that, a new day began.

I walked through town and noticed how prevalent joy seemed to be with the citizens of Concord. As I approached the well in the center of town, I saw a tall, energetic, athletic-looking girl with long, dark hair that flowed freely as she stretched. A bit older than I, she looked familiar, though I couldn't remember her name. It seemed, from her demeanor, that she was preparing for some vigorous training.

"A good day to be outside, yeah?" I called out to her.

The girl smiled and jogged towards me. "Yes! Perfect weather for a good run! Any weather is good weather to run, really!"

Her energy startled me. "And of rain? Or snow?" I asked her playfully.

"Oh, that just makes the run more interesting! I appreciate a sunny day as much as a rainy or snowy one! Any day I can run is a great day to me!" I wondered if even the gods could muster enough power to stop her from running.

"Remind me your name?" I asked, embarrassed.

"Helene!" she called over her shoulder, already running away from me.

"Why do you love running so much, Helene?" I yelled to her as she quickly sped down the street.

"I will tell you if you can keep up, Tortoise!" she laughed, sprinting away.

I knew that I was not in any kind of shape to chase Helene, but my curiosity could not refuse a simple challenge. With an energetic shout, I started to move my legs and thus, the chase began.

Buildings and people became blurs as we raced down the various streets and alleyways of Concord. After a few minutes, I had caught up with her, but I could barely muster enough breath to speak. Helene looked over at me, giggled, and then sped by me once again. As we approached the town gate, I took a deep breath and used what energy I had left to throw myself into a sprint. We both rushed towards the gate, the desire to win fueling us. Right before reaching the finish line, my body began to cramp, and my lungs failed to give me another full breath. I fell to the ground while Helene flew by me with the utmost ease and grace. Although I had given it my all, I was defeated. I remained on my hands and knees, taking in as much air as I possibly could with each breath. The ground felt warm beneath my palms.

"Slowpoke!" Helene yelled with a grin. She didn't look as if she'd run a race at all. I rolled to my back, still attempting to recover from our friendly competition. To anyone watching, I am sure I looked like I was in my final death throes.

"Helene...I...haven't...run...in so long..."

"*That* is why I love running," Helene said cheerfully.

"What do you mean?"

"I mean the way you are now, exhausted and in pain. You will grow stronger and faster from it the next time! You must feel excited about that!" When she put it that way, it made more sense. I recalled my battles with Raptor and Bella, as well as the training I had done with my sword; all the pain brought new knowledge and experience. Bertrand's symphony began to play in my mind.

"You really are a great runner. Do you mind teaching me a few things?" I asked Helene graciously. I had thought myself fit; I knew now that I'd been wrong.

"Of course! Just don't overwork yourself this time, okay?" I nodded my head as we walked back towards the fountain. I glanced at Helene as we went and wondered what drove her to run as much as she did.

"You must be training for a competition," I ventured.

"Not just *a* competition, Tortoise. I am training for *all* competitions." Helene put her hands on her hips in a triumphant fashion.

"Any competition in particular?" I asked.

"No, not yet. The last time I competed, I lost by a huge margin. If you think I am fast, there are many, many people faster than

I am." Helene raised her eyebrows and continued to walk. After our race, I couldn't imagine anyone faster than Helene. Her face remained stern as she reminisced on her last competition. I knew her thirst for victory would not be sated until she was the very best.

My legs wobbled as we reached the fountain. My mouth felt like an arid desert that had not seen rain in months. With all the energy I could muster, I dipped the bucket into the well and got as much water as it could possibly hold. I had not known how fast I could drink a bucket of water until today, and as I slurped down the refreshing liquid, I noticed Helene laughing between my ravenous slurps.

"That is water, Tortoise. You've never had any, have you?" She continued to laugh at my incredible thirst.

"This liquid you call water is delicious!" I said to her jokingly.

"So you wish to learn how to run." I could tell by the newly serious tone of her voice that she was passionate about teaching others her art.

"Well, I am already a good walker; I suppose learning how to run effectively would be helpful."

"Running is all about consistency, Tortoise. It is an art you must practice every day to become even moderately proficient. If I teach you some of my secrets, you need to promise me that you will practice them every day." Helene's eyes burned like forest fires as she talked.

"I will practice your secrets every day, and maybe one day I will beat you in a race!" I enthused.

"That is the spirit!" Helene said, smiling.

"Before you run, make sure to stretch. There is no use in running if you are just going to injure yourself."

Helene motioned for me to begin now. I reached down to touch my toes.

"Not like that! You are too rigid. Try again, but this time, move more gracefully. Give your muscles time to warm up."

I touched my toes again, this time moving more slowly,

thinking about each individual muscle in my leg as I went.

"That is better. Now I want you to focus on your breathing. You must make every breath count as you run. Remember: consistency, Tortoise."

I took a deep breath, taking in as much air as I possibly could.

"Stop! We aren't training for a dive, Tortoise!" Helene yelled. I exhaled suddenly and waited for further instruction. "Breathe normally but consistently. Let your lungs fill with air naturally."

I took what Helene said into consideration and took a breath again, except this time I made sure to inhale calmly. As I completed my breath, I could see Helene smile. "Good job, Tortoise. Now I want you to show me how you run." Helene pointed her finger, telling me to start. I shuffled my feet and ran over to the edge of the town square, remembering to breathe efficiently. As I ran back to Helene, she shook her head disapprovingly.

"The breathing was good, but your steps were all over the place."

I was surprised by all the subtle nuances that went into running. I had run many times in my life before, but after working with Helene, I knew that I had been doing it all wrong.

There is always room for improvement in life, I thought as Helene began to speak again.

"Make your steps consistent with your breaths; this will help you run longer distances without feeling as fatigued. Consistency, Tortoise!"

Helene's conviction inspired me to strive for perfection in my steps. This time, I focused on making all my steps more fluid, making sure that my strides were neither too long nor too short. As I ran, I could feel more energy with each stride than I had before. I smiled as I ran back to Helene.

"This tortoise may turn into a hare!" Helene laughed, clapping her hands. "Well, that is your lesson for today; I am glad I could help you!"

I grinned as I began to feel some of Helene's unstoppable

energy flow through me. "I appreciate all your help, Helene. I wish you the best of luck in all your competitions." After some practice, I knew I would want to show Helene how much I had improved.

"Tortoise!" Helene yelled, making me jump. "Fortune favors consistency above all other qualities. What it is that you are chasing, never stop running. The finish line is sometimes closer than we expect."

I shook Helene's hand, and, like a hare sprinting across the grasslands, she was off.

"I expect to race you the next time we bump into each other!" she yelled, zooming down the streets of Concord once more.

Consistency. What a powerful quality to possess.

When I had reached Bastion and walked through its gates, I sensed a shift in its atmosphere. Usually, the city walls provided a feeling of comfort and safety, but there was an unusual, and fearful, commotion today.

"Excuse me," I said to the guard. "Do you know what's going on?"

His armor clanked as he walked over to me. "Caliburn, Bastion's finest national treasure, was pilfered from its resting place last night, and the soldiers guarding it were killed mercilessly. Those soldiers could only have been overwhelmed by a group of skilled thieves—maybe four or five. Today, Bastion's citizens all fear for their safety."

While I did not know much about the legend of Caliburn, I knew that a group of thieves willing to steal such a revered artifact would be hunted until they were all captured and executed. The legends say that anyone who wraps their fingers around Caliburn's timeless handle undeservingly will find himself unfathomably peerless in skill and strength. I had always been skeptical of Caliburn's legendary abilities, but after meeting The Sage, I understood that there was likely to be some truth behind any myth.

"All soldiers are on high alert, and a tremendous bounty sits on the group that stole the sword. I would assume that every mercenary worth his salt is out there, chasing those marauders as we speak." The guard sighed and returned to his slouched position, his armor clicking and clanking as he moved lethargically, finally using his sword to prop himself up once more.

Still as lively as ever, I thought to myself, giggling as I remembered what Bone Rattle had said a few days ago.

The guard's words reminded me of Raptor and Bone Rattle; I knew that if any duo could return the sword to Bastion, it would be them.

The stones beneath my feet blended with the gray buildings, which in turn blended with the bulwark of weathered walls around me. The uniformity of tone was disorienting. The citizens with their pops of color who usually broke the chromatic monotony were absent today, replaced by gray-uniformed soldiers who seemed to disappear into the city's muted palette.

As I stopped to think about what had happened that day, I met a young soldier's eyes. And indescribable pain lay behind his unflinching demeanor.

His gaze intensified; I could see his hand move to the hilt of his sword. My hairs stood on end, and my body began to prepare itself for a possible altercation.

"You. Why do you look at me the way you do?" The soldier's eyes turned ever more aggressive as he stalked towards me.

I had no answer.

"You seem suspicious; are you one of the curs that murdered my brother? Answer me!"

The pain I saw behind this soldier's raging eyes stemmed from a great loss. I held my ground and tried to speak once more, but I was still at a loss for words.

"I'm sorry..." Before I could finish, the soldier's sword whizzed out of its leather scabbard.

"*Sorry*? My brother described you to me before he died in my arms. Now *you* will die, impaled upon my sword. You can apologize to my brother when you meet him in the next life!" the soldier yelled. I could see that fear and anger bubbled in his spirit.

Those thieves…. They have stolen a lot more than a sword from this city, I thought.

"Soldier, I am not—"

The soldier's flashing blade interrupted me; I dodged out of the way of his blow.

"Draw your weapon or die like a coward—your choice!" the soldier roared angrily.

With a sigh, I drew my sword and prepared to protect my life.

The soldier's style was unlike any I had previously encountered—while Raptor's style was slow and controlled and Bella's was fast, unrestrained, and ruthless, I could sense a practiced uniformity behind his moves. That, and the soldier's youth led me to believe that this was his first fight outside of sparring.

He once again swung his sword recklessly; I parried his blow and dodged away.

"Calm down! I am not one of the marauders that stole the sword!" I yelled, worried.

"Best me in combat, then! If you survive, you'll have the chance to explain yourself!" he shrieked, loosing venomous rage from his eyes. His fury reminded me of what I had felt during my first fight. *I was stupid to assume his brashness was a weakness*, I thought worriedly. The sheer flurry of blows caused me to crumple; in an instant I toppled to the ground.

The crimson blood now gushing from my body turned burgundy when it reached the cold gray stone beneath me. I felt a burning sensation on the side of my abdomen. As my fingers grazed the cut, I felt that, while it was not deep, it would continue to bleed if I did not act quickly.

"Well, is that all out of you? The only way you could have defeated my brother was through a sneak attack. Make peace with any gods you worship; you will see them soon enough!" The soldier stood over me and swung his sword at my throat.

In that moment, I felt no fear but, rather, an instinct to remain alive. I had come too far in my journey to be mistaken for a thief.

I rolled away from his swing, wincing in pain as my cut touched the cold ground. I managed to get back to my feet, but seconds later, I was knocked down once more when I attempted to parry one of his powerful blows. The wound at my side continued to bleed. My vision grew wobbly. Finishing this fight quickly was my only option.

"Soldier! Stay your sword!" a gruff voice crackled through the air, causing the soldier to pause in his onslaught.

I looked up in a daze. The man wore brilliant armor that I remembered seeing before. Our eyes met. The prominent scar on his cheek told me just who it was, standing before us.

"I believe you were told to remain on high alert and report all suspicious activity to your commanding officer—correct me if I am wrong!"

The soldier quickly took a knee and bowed his head. "No, sir, General Frederick, sir!"

Frederick glared at the soldier with disappointment. "Return to the barracks immediately! Inform your commanding officer that I expect to see you in my office!" Frederick howled. His commands rumbled through the buildings that surrounded us.

"Sir, yes, sir!" With a defeated look, the soldier took off in a sprint.

I felt no anger towards him; I knew that everyone in The Stronghold felt in danger today, especially those who had lost someone to the thieves. Breathing heavily, my consciousness began to fade.

"Let's get you to the infirmary. We must get this..." Frederick's voice trailed off as the world around me faded away to darkness.

Much later, I slowly opened my eyes and looked around. Empty beds lined the quiet room to which I'd been brought.

I heard a gentle voice from the doorway say, "Ah, you are awake," and I turned my head to see a physician walking to the bed to sit in a chair close to the wall.

"There was only minor blood loss associated with your injury. When Frederick brought you here, we gave you strong pain relievers, and then we sealed the wound with a hot iron. You passed out from the sight of blood leaving your body; this is not an uncommon occurrence."

I was relieved, but then I began to panic, for it was dark outside, and I had yet to visit the tree.

"When will I be able to leave?" I asked the physician nervously.

"I have been instructed to watch over you until Frederick returns. Until then, you must rest. We have prepared some soup to replenish your energy. I will get you some water, as well." He got up from his chair and left the room to fetch the soup and water. I wondered how long it would be before Frederick returned.

"If you fail or forget to tend to the plant for just one day, it will wither and die, and your chances of gaining eternal life will wither away as well," The Sage had told me. I sighed uncomfortably. Wincing, I got up from the bed. My body stung where the wound had been sealed. I was met by stiff plate mail as I attempted to exit the room.

"Where do you plan to go, boy?" Frederick's eyes glimmered softly in the dim lighting; two slate orbs well weathered by a lifetime of storms.

"Um, I just need to take care of something tonight."

"Take care of what, boy? You are injured; can it not wait until tomorrow?" Frederick's gaze grew ever more suspicious as we stood in the doorway.

"No, sir. I am sorry, but I must leave soon. I appreciate your help earlier today, but I have an errand I must tend to." My voice cracked and my lips quivered as The Sage's magic spoke for me.

Frederick's hand firmly grasped the hilt of his sword. "Errand? At this hour? Your words do not match your heart."

I felt entombed. Frederick's glare petrified every muscle in my body.

"I must be on my way now, Frederick."

Frederick's palm pushed me to the ground abruptly. "Take a seat on that bed, unless you would rather share a few words with my blade."

I got up from the floor slowly and sat on the bed. Not even Frederick trusted me now.

"You know by now that The Stronghold's most valuable national treasure was pilfered by a group of bandits last night. Not only that, but now four soldiers have lost their lives, as well. Caliburn is valuable, yes, but what is equally valuable are my brothers-in-arms and the well-being of the citizens for whose protection I have dedicated my life. I believe in fair trials, and you will be innocent until you are proven guilty. But: we checked your bags after your scuffle with one of our soldiers, assuming you to be a mercenary. However, your bag held no warrants. A curious map, a dozen gold pieces, and a jar of water is all we found. You travel with a weapon, and you are not a mercenary. Most citizens, especially those of Bastion and the surrounding towns, do not carry a weapon. Local militia will have them, yes, but not in a scabbard by their side. The physical similarities between you and the description of one of the thieves are uncanny. And now, your behavior about where you must go. I will ask this once: be honest and specific about where you intend to go and your business traveling through Bastion earlier today. If you are not, I will be forced to use more...unsavory methods to extract the information I need."

It was impossible for me to be completely honest about where I intended to go after leaving the infirmary. Trying to explain would be futile.

"Frederick, please believe me when I say that the errand I must attend to is of the utmost importance," I said wearily. Frederick remained silent and stared at me. I remained silent as well. *Patience*, I thought as I waited for Frederick to speak. The silence in the room made time stretch on and on without end. *I wonder if this is how Bella feels, always surrounded by quiet.* Frederick sighed.

"All right, boy. You have until the ring of the clocktower to be back in this room. If you are not, you will be chased by every mercenary and soldier in the land until you are caught. Is this clear to you?" Frederick's stare hardened as he explained the terms of my absence. "You have about half of the hour left to take care of whatever this business of yours is. Your fate will be decided when the bell rings." Frederick nodded his head towards the door after he finished speaking.

"Yes sir," I said as I got off the bed. I shivered as I walked across the room, my steps echoing against the muted walls of the infirmary.

Silence engulfed the entirety of Bastion. The cool night air helped somewhat to ease the tension I felt as I prepared to trek across the city and tend to the tree. "It normally takes me about half an hour to cross Bastion," I sighed despondently as I thought of the distance. "I've made it to the tree for the past three days; I can't give up now." Suddenly, I was overcome with the unstoppable energy I had felt earlier today.

"Consistency, Tortoise!" Helene's words pranced like jackrabbits in my mind. The night air filled my body with hope with each breath I took. The pounding of my boots disturbed the silence that hung about the moonlit streets.

I stopped after dashing down a dim alleyway that went on into the dark of the night. "Before you run, make sure to stretch. There is no use in running if you are just going to injure yourself." I repeated Helene's words to myself. Focusing intently on every muscle, I proceeded to limber up. If I sustained another injury, making it to the tree would be impossible. My spirit was tethered to the tree, and I could sense that it was in great distress. *Now, I want you to focus on your breathing. You must make every breath count as your run. Remember: consistency, Tortoise.* The run grew more difficult as I sprinted down the lightless streets. The cut on my abdomen burned and ached. Each breath I took was calculated and precious. *The moon is watching me and no one else.* The stone gave way to dirt beneath my feet, and I knew now that I was in no position to stop and rest.

Make your steps consistent with your breaths; this will help you run longer distances without feeling as fatigued. Consistency, Tortoise! The further I ran down the hollow, the darker the world around me became. Fire began to build in my legs; each stride was more painful than the last.

I visualized the tree, knowing to keep my body aligned to the goal in my mind aligned in my mind. I thought about when I had first met The Sage. The Sage had seen my entire story before I had ever seen him. He knew how this whole adventure would turn out. All I knew was that, at the end of it all, eternity would be there waiting for me.

As my mind wandered and my body sprinted, I finally reached the tree's birthplace. Reaching into my sack, I felt around for the water. When I didn't feel it, I began to frantically run my hands through every inch of my bag, falling to my knees from the extreme agony of my feet and legs. Sweat dripped from my face and made mild tapping noises as it hit the ground.

After shaking out the contents of my bag, I realized that I had failed. Gazing at the tree in despair, tortured by the physical pain from my legs and the mental anguish of failure, I collapsed.

"Sage, I failed myself and you.... What was the point of this journey, if this is how it was all going to turn out?"

DAY 5:

SILVER HOWL

"You know, whelp, you are real lucky we are the mercenaries that found you here."

I jumped up from my slumber, gasping at the lingering soreness in my legs and around my wound. "Raptor! How did you find me?"

Suddenly, I remembered the tree. I looked up and, by some stroke of luck, the tree had grown again. The roots of the tree were now thick and dug into the soft soil like fingers flowing through sand. Its branches reached for the sky, and its trunk had become so large and tough that even the sharpest axe swung by the strongest man would leave nothing but a nick on its surface.

"Whelp! You look like you just saw an apparition!" Raptor remarked.

"I am just really tired and surprised to see the both of you again," I said calmly.

"A warrant was put out on you last night. When I read the description, I was baffled; I knew you were far too weak to kill another man, let alone steal the finest sword in the land. Rattle and I were tipped off by some of the night watch around town that you had run towards this location. You are stupid to have run from Frederick, no matter what your errand was."

I nodded my head reluctantly. "I guess you and Bone Rattle will be taking me back into town, then?" I asked wearily.

"What else? The reward for your capture could fill even the largest coffer! I've been needing a new axe, and my boots have gotten awfully beat up here recently..." Bone Rattle giggled, his laughter reminding me of how close to death I had come.

"We will turn you in, but you will have to explain yourself to Frederick. Neither I nor Rattle will be able to do much, other than tell him what a declawed kitten you are," Raptor chuckled gruffly. I gulped.

My legs burned, as if someone had submerged me hip-deep into a pot of boiling water. *It means that the way you are now, exhausted and in some minor pain. You will grow stronger and faster from it the next time! You must feel excited about that.* Helene had taught me about more than just running. It hadn't occurred to me until then just how much I had survived in the past few days. I would never have thought that I could do so much.

I limped as Raptor and Bone Rattle escorted me back to Frederick.

The city seemed a bit livelier than it had the day before. Soldiers stood guard at every corner of Bastion, resembling pebbles scattered across a dusky canyon. As we continued towards Frederick's office, mercenaries of all types rushed down the streets.

"They must have updated reports of the thieves," Raptor discerned.

"Any luck chasing them?" I asked.

"Well, we found one in the middle of nowhere and, once we realized who he was, we knew we had wasted our time," Bone Rattle cackled sarcastically.

"As far as I'm aware, there are four thieves: three men and a woman. One obviously looks like you. The other two men are burlier types. One of the men has longer, blond hair and a tattoo of a hawk on his right arm. The other man is a shorter, stockier type with curly brown hair and a few missing teeth. Finally, the girl is said to be the most dangerous of the three. An unexpected one as well; you would probably miss her in a crowd of people." I could see that Raptor was intent on hunting down the thieves and retrieving Caliburn.

"Do you believe the stories behind the sword?" I inquired of Raptor.

"The legends surrounding that old sword do not scare me, and I do not care about retrieving it. I pursue warrants for the rewards, not the glory." Raptor gazed forward towards Frederick's office warmly; I wondered how both men would feel, seeing each other again after so long. We stepped into the barracks, our footsteps echoing across the building eerily. *All the soldiers must be out on patrol*, I thought. The building was constructed of worn and tarnished wood; its appearance revealed its age. Through a doorway towards the back of the building, we saw Frederick working intently at his desk. Walking across the barracks floor, I looked at Raptor's scar-covered face. His nose had a particularly nasty scar that seemed to have been there for years.

"Where did you get that scar on your nose?" I asked Raptor.

"From the most dangerous warrior I have ever faced."

My imagination ran wild—I pictured Raptor fighting the most skilled criminal from a foreign land. "What was his name? Did you kill him in battle? Was he a thief? A mass murderer?" I was extremely interested in hearing all of Raptor's stories, and this one was no different.

"You just never stop asking questions, do you, whelp? First off, he was a she. This woman was scarier than any other person I had ever fought in my life, more fearsome than Frederick, even."

I had never thought I would see Raptor, the greatest mercenary in the land, scared. My mind raced and sweat dripped from my forehead.

"Who was she then? Her skill in combat must have been formidable to have left such a scar on your nose." I was dying to hear about Raptor's encounter with this terrible foe.

"The woman was my mother."

Bone Rattle began to laugh hysterically as I looked at Raptor, confused.

"Your mother?" I asked.

"Yes. Long ago, Mother told me to stop thieving or else she would put me out on the street. I was younger at the time; this happened a year before I encountered Frederick. I told her that if she wanted to make me stop, she would have to do it by force. After I let those foolish words escape from my mouth, Mother boiled with an anger hotter than the most scorching sun. She immediately took one of the pans she had been cooking with and smacked me square in the face. The edge of the pan sliced straight across the bridge of my nose and left the nasty beauty mark you see before you. That was the last time I ever saw my mother. Every time I run my fingers over that scar now, I feel remorse for not treating her better. She was the only one who saw me as a child and not a criminal. I will never have the chance to say I'm sorry, but at least I have the chance to be a better man than the one she knew."

Raptor smiled, something I had only seen him do once before, and I realized something—this fearsome and battle-scarred warrior was, it turned out, simply a grown boy who wanted nothing more than to make amends with his mother.

We had reached Frederick's office while Raptor was speaking, and I now looked around. The walls were filled with a variety of books. His desk was plain yet functional. He was dressed differently today, wearing a beige dress shirt under a dark cotton cuirass. Frederick seemed to be a man of utility, preferring effective simplicity over useless complexity.

"You are quite lucky we caught your doppelganger yesterday, boy. Had we found you first, you would most certainly be sitting in a jail cell being interrogated by my most ruthless detectives." I gulped as Frederick glared at me. "I am still curious as to why you had to leave the infirmary last night."

Bone Rattle giggled quietly to himself before saying, "The

child was probably out chasing fireflies and got too tuckered out to run back." I scowled.

"This whelp is one of those soft types. I am sure he was tending to some flowers out where we found him." Without realizing it, Raptor was speaking quite truthfully.

"Well, what was it boy, were you chasing fireflies or watering flowers?" Frederick squinted his eyes in an agitated way.

"Flowers, sir. I am quite secretive about it. I will be teased if anyone finds out; I am very insecure about it."

"A man does not care for what he may be teased. He does as he pleases to the best of his ability. You remember that well, boy. Your insecurities could have gotten you seriously injured, or worse."

"Yes, sir," I said, nodding my head.

"Aquila, I have heard much about your heroics over the years." Frederick turned his head to Raptor and nodded deferentially.

"And I have not heard that name in so many years." Raptor gazed at Frederick with the same deferential look.

"I trust that you will find Caliburn and the thieves who stole her from her resting place."

Bone Rattle scoffed. "I had a mind to catch all four of the rodents, but three will make for a good story, I suppose."

Frederick felt the scar on his face and began to speak. "You mercenaries may be on your way now. Aquila, keep your sword arm in good shape; I would like to see who's the better man after all of these years."

Raptor smirked. "You have yourself a deal, old man. Thank you again."

Frederick gave Raptor a friendly nod, and the three of us turned to go.

"Not so fast, boy, you aren't leaving just yet." I turned around abruptly. Raptor and Bone Rattle continued on their way.

"Yes, sir?" I asked timidly.

"How do you know those mercenaries?"

"I was traveling through the forest one day, and I was accosted by some bandits. Raptor and Bone Rattle had been hunting those bandits for some time and saved me from being killed that day." Frederick nodded his head as he pulled my sword from under the table.

"Civilians do not normally carry weapons by their sides," Frederick pointed out.

"After my encounter with the bandits, the mercenaries took me to the infirmary to get my wounds treated. On the way, we ran into a traveling salesman. Raptor bought me that sword." Frederick remained silent in a way that I knew he wanted me to continue my story. "After he bought me the sword, we sparred. I had never been formally trained to use a sword, but Raptor said that the best fighting comes from instinct. I won, but I knew that he had been going easy the whole time."

Frederick took a sip from the cup sitting on his desk.

"Aquila is the most formidable warrior on the continent. The scar you see on my cheek came from him."

I remembered Raptor's story about their battle. "You keep saying Aquila; why does he not go by that name anymore?" I asked.

"Aquila was once a feared criminal around these parts. He was quite the robber, looting houses and businesses alike. When he was apprehended, many of the men that sat in our city council wanted him executed. I could see the spark in the young man's eyes, though. I appealed to have him serve a severe prison sentence instead. Aquila was a swordsman unlike any other his age at the time. I remember him entering tournaments designed for adults, because they were the only ones that provided him with a challenge. Unfortunately, as he grew older, he began to take on more unsavory practices. I was always intrigued by the idea of testing his abilities against mine, but I never thought it would happen the way it did. I assume that once Aquila was freed from prison, he wished to leave that part of his life behind him, name and all."

I thought about what Frederick had said. Raptor's mother wasn't the only person who had always seen him as a child. "Frederick, Raptor said that during my battle with him, I showed an animalistic fury he had seen only once before. Was he talking about you?" I felt uneasy asking, as it reminded me of how I had lost control over myself.

"Boy...you see, there is an animal that resides within each of us. These animals are powerful, vicious, and dangerous beyond reason. Some people are friends with their animals from birth. They know their animals well and respect them for their strength and ferocity. I met my wolf as a pup, and we have been companions ever since. Other people are born with an animal that they cannot or choose not to tame. Aquila was one such person, a long time ago. Once he learned to tame the predator that resides in the depths of his soul, a new person was able to take flight—the Merciless Eagle. There are a few people, however, who never met their animals when they were born. For a long time, these people venture through life, oblivious to the power that exists within them. Then, at a certain point in their lives, they reach an obstacle they cannot reasonably overcome on their own. Unbeknownst to them, the animal within them awakens to conquer what they cannot conquer alone. This rage, this fury...it scared you."

I was scared, but now I understood a lot more. Speaking to Frederick reassured me that it was not I who had almost killed Raptor, but the animal that lives within me. "So how do I go about taming the animal?" I knew now why Raptor had stressed the importance of fighting from instinct.

"No animal learns behind the bars of a cage. You must loose the beast from your heart and teach it to share its strength with you." Frederick continued to work on papers. Sunlight poked through the window behind him and tickled my face pleasantly. Watching Frederick work, I thought about my own abilities and the days to come. I had trained a fair amount since I had started on my journey four days earlier. Even so, fighting Raptor, Bella, and the young soldier had taught me that I still had much to learn before I could become an accomplished swordsman.

"Come." Frederick got up from his chair.

By the look in his eyes, I knew he was preparing his mind for battle. Before leaving the office, he motioned towards my sword. I grabbed it quickly, and we proceeded.

"My intuition tells me that there is more to you and why you are here today." Frederick looked at me in a discerning way. We stood in the middle of the barracks now. Creaks could be heard all throughout the building as the wind blew outside.

"What do you mean?" I asked Frederick, confused.

"You...you chase after something, I can tell. I know you didn't leave the infirmary last night to water flowers. You are on a journey to do something greater than that.... And I have become a part of your journey to prepare you for what you chase." Frederick whipped his sword out of its scabbard, the weapon making a howling noise as it exited its leathern sheathe.

"Come boy! Show me the animal that lives deep within your heart!" Frederick roared.

I nodded sternly; Raptor had helped me unleash my inner instincts, and now Frederick would help me tame them.

I listened to my sword as I unsheathed it—every weapon has a voice of its own.

Frederick bowed to me. Bowing back, I saw that his eyes blazed like volcanic rock. I stood my guard. Frederick waved his sword gracefully, circling around me slowly.

Resembling a wolf baring its fangs as it hunts its prey. I shuddered. In an instant, he lunged. I parried his strike and fell backwards onto the floor.

His speed! Even though he's older, he's faster than anyone else. I got up from the barracks floor.

Frederick continued to circle around me. His style was unlike any other I had come across so far.

I stood my guard once again, looking for an opening.

Without hesitation, I faked one way and then lunged the other, swinging towards him aggressively. Frederick moved—effortlessly, it appeared—away and my sword slammed on to the ground. Capitalizing on my error, Frederick lunged towards me again, pointing his sword dangerously close to my face.

"Try again, boy. You won't come close to beating me with

moves like that."

I blindly swung at Frederick again, hoping the spontaneity of my strike would catch him off guard. Yet again, Frederick parried my blow. Advancing towards him, I thrusted my sword continuously. Frederick parried each blow with ease, and with excessive force, pushed me to the ground. My body hit the planks of the barracks floor once more, as the thud of my fall echoed across the empty building.

"That is the second time you have fallen, boy; if this were a true battle, I would have killed you twice by now. Come!" Frederick pointed his sword in my direction.

I thought of everything I had learned from the manual in the library, as well as from Raptor. I attacked Frederick with all the strength I could muster, wildly swinging and dodging his counterattacks to try and find and opening.

"Struggle away! You cannot defeat me alone! Unleash the power within you! Trust it! Trust the beast that lies dormant within your soul!"

I continued to weather Frederick's attacks. After trading a multitude of blows, I finally saw an opening. Frederick stumbled backwards, and as he did, I made one swift lunge towards him. As Frederick recovered from his stumble, he ducked and swung towards my blade, knocking it out of my hands. The sound of metal rattled throughout the barracks.

"You continue to fight alone, and now without a sword!" Frederick laughed as he continued to swing towards me. Dodging his blows, I began to feel enveloped by anger.

I fell back.

Frederick came to a standstill, as my vision faded away to an alternate realm. Opening my eyes, I saw within the shroud of darkness a cat with radiant white fur. I looked around the room, wondering where I was. *I am certainly not dead.* I got up from the ground slowly and began to walk towards the cat, feeling strangely at ease in the curious shadows that surrounded me. "Hello little—aagh!" The cat jumped up and bit my fingers before I could reach down to pet its glorious fur.

"You! You can ask for permission before petting me! You are aware of that, right?" I hopped back in surprise; this cat could speak!

"Where am I, cat?" I asked the little creature.

"Where you are does not matter much. What matters is *why* you are here." The cat said, pithily.

"Well, why am I here?"

"I am just as confused as you are. You have never asked me for help before. I couldn't help but come out to play once, but you were not ready."

I thought about what the cat was saying and realized where I was. The beast Frederick had talked about before was not metaphorical at all!

"Cat, someone told me today that there are some challenges I will meet in life that I will not be able to conquer again." The cat meowed.

"Yes, just as there are challenges I cannot conquer without you. We are one and the same, you and I."

"I need your help. I know my journey will become more difficult, and I would like to see it to its conclusion, with you beside me." I kneeled as I spoke.

"I thirst for adventure! You have gone all these years without any danger, any thrills! I will help you, only if you promise to continue finding us grander feats to overcome! Just as relaxation is calming to you, excitement is calming to me!" The cat meowed with all the ferocity of a lion.

"All right, you have a deal." I shook the cat's paw, and it purred happily.

I opened my eyes, time moving again at its normal pace. I rolled under Frederick's swing and promptly reclaimed my blade. As I stood up, I could feel the same primal energy I had felt in my battle with Raptor. I recognized that I now had control over this feral force blazing from my inner being.

"Don't hold back!" Frederick yelled.

"Yes, sir!"

Giving him an incredible exercise was all I could focus on

now.

I charged towards Frederick, letting my instincts, rather than my mind, guide me.

As we exchanged blows, I knew I wasn't fighting this battle alone anymore. Swinging to defend all his blows, I sensed an opening that I could not capitalize on by myself. Working with the cat made me more nimble in body and confident in spirit. I realized that the cat moved faster than I could think, teaching me to follow my instincts rather than my thoughts.

"There it is! Dance with your companion! Allow it to unlock your true potential!" Frederick yelled as we fought. Parrying one of the many blows he threw at me, I pushed his sword out of the way, using all the power the cat had shared with me.

"Now!" I roared. The tip of my sword was now only a hair's width away from Frederick's nose.

"All of these years, you have buried your real abilities. Thank you for the fierce match, boy!" Frederick, breathing hard like I was, bowed to me. Bowing back, I smiled. "There is still much for you to learn, but I have no doubt in my mind that you were born to learn the ways of the sword. Let me instill in you some of what I have learned—if you have time, of course."

I nodded and continued to listen to his advice. I had made not one, but two new friends today. There was a piece of myself that had been locked away, and I would have never known it if it weren't for the tutelage given to me by the Wolf and the Eagle.

"Boy, when I was your age, I wanted nothing more than to make this city proud. I have served the people in my life under many different titles. To the citizens of this city, I have been a soldier and now a general. To my family, I have been a husband and a father. To you, boy, I have been a teacher. There is a level of responsibility that comes with each."

I thought about what Frederick was saying for a few minutes as we took the time to drink some water and recuperate from our training session. "What do you mean? What sort of responsibility?" I asked.

"The responsibility to be the most you can possibly be to

those people in your life. I am sure you recognize that you are a son to your parents, a friend to those you have met on your journey, and a student to me. Just as it is my duty to teach you what I can before you leave, it is your duty to learn as much as you can."

I knew what he was saying was true, but it was easy to forget at times.

Outside of the windows of the barracks I saw the sun begin to draw its rays from the sullen gray stones that made up the city.

"Frederick, I appreciate everything you have taught me. You showed me how to master my instincts, and you taught me techniques I could have never learned, had you not shown me."

Frederick's laugh rumbled through the barracks like an erupting volcano.

"Thank *you*, boy!"

I scratched my head. "For what?"

"You gave me the opportunity to exercise patience and understanding in a difficult situation. You helped me remember what a good match feels like. You allowed me to share my knowledge with you, not just in swordplay, but in other ways, as well."

I had never had someone thank me for the opportunities I had given them. And I was elated that I had given him a good fight.

"I am glad I could help you in some way, Frederick," I said.

"Boy, I know not where you will go moving forward, but I know that what you move towards is very important to you. Remember your duties well. At times, it may be difficult, but you must continue to press forward. Trust in your instincts. What separates us from the beasts that populate this world is that while we know what we must do in depths of our heart, we continue to think and ruminate over the possibilities. We do not trust ourselves enough to decide, and that leaves room for errors and mistakes. Remain in tune with the instincts that have always resided within you, and that path you must travel will become clear." I sensed that Frederick knew it was time for me to continue my journey.

"You have seemed so calm, so secure for the time I have known you. Now I know why."

"Go on, boy, and take this." Frederick pulled a few papers from his pocket, as well as a small golden pin in the shape of a castle. I remembered that Raptor and Bone Rattle both wore castle pins on their clothes. "This paper grants you the option to chase warrants, should you choose to do so. This one here is specific to the thieves who have stolen the sword. This pin, in the shape of our impregnable city, is a symbol showing that you have demonstrated the qualities necessary to be employed as a warrior in the Stronghold of Bastion. Wear it proudly. Whatever you wish to pursue in life, know that you may always serve this city and the people who live within it."

I bowed to Frederick for the last time, and he bowed back to me. Today I became an honorary mercenary. While I was afraid of what this meant for the future, a part of me was excited. I knew that soon, my destiny would meet me. No amount of fear would defer whatever reality awaited me.

I walked out of the barracks with the golden castle pin displayed on the left side of my shirt. I stood in front of the creaking wooden building for a few more minutes. The setting sun did much to energize me, as its light gently washed over the city.

My mind wandered to Bella. I had thought of her many times since I had met her a few days ago. I envisioned bringing her to meet my mother once my journey was over.

Thank you, Sage, for all of this. Without him, I never would have met such a beautiful individual. Frederick's words caused me to reflect deeply. My duty to Bella was to find her and be her companion for the rest of our days. We could experience every inch of the world; she would never have to be alone with me by her side.

After stretching and breathing in the cool air of the twilit city, I started my walk to the tree.

Reaching the tree's home. I looked around. This area had become filled with increasing life as the days had progressed, and now there were various bushes, vines, and flowers acting as a cloak of sorts. The tree rested in the middle of it all.

I moved closer to it, its branches waving methodically

with the passing winds. I poured the contents of the jar I had with me all around the tree. I sat down with my arms cradling my knees. The tree grew to enormous proportions, covering the entirety of the sky above me with its powerful, intricate branches. As the sun continued to set, I thought about the trials I would face moving forward.

In two days, I would see The Sage again. In two days, my expiration date would expire. All the time in the world would belong to me: this became more and more exciting as I thought about how much more interesting each day had been since that first one, five days before.

DAY 6:
THUNDER

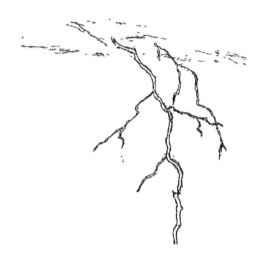

    The sun was obscured by an army of dark clouds that slowly floated across the sky. I stood at the edge of the forest, stretching my muscles as my mind chased all kinds of ideas: Caliburn, the thieves, and their motives for stealing such a supposedly powerful artifact. Why did they pick to steal the most prized item in the land? Surely most people know of Caliburn and its importance; it would be difficult to sell such a thing to a merchant or even on the black market. Anyone stupid enough to purchase the sword would be hunted down.

    As I pondered the thieves and their motives, it occurred to me that no one seemed to believe the myths about Caliburn, however desperate they might be to get it back. However fantastic the myths about The Sage had become over the years, they could not match the truth of his power. I feared the same would prove correct about Caliburn.

My hands shook. The air carried a baleful energy that caused me to tremble. *What could this mean?* The sounds of the forest slowly came to a halt, as I began to train, focusing on the skills I had learned the day before. The cool breeze that blew through the trees whispered calming thoughts into my ears throughout my training. To conclude the session, I ran towards the end of the forest, concentrating on what Helene had shown me. I wanted now to perfect not just my swordsmanship, but my fitness, as well. My body was in constant pain from all of the unaccustomed work, but my mind was slowly being tempered now by the will to reach my goal.

I knew that Bertrand could tell me more about Caliburn. I hoped that, after talking with him, I could help Frederick and Raptor reclaim the sword and restore peace to Bastion. I walked through the city, taking note of all the robust stone buildings that stood next to each other. "A small house, with circular windows and an intricate wooden door," I murmured. After some searching, I finally came upon Bertrand's home. I knocked on the door and wondered how he had been over the last few days.

"Stranger! I hoped to see you again! Come in!" Bertrand said, after he had swung the door open. The smell of ginger tea emanated from the doorway, piquing my thirst. The room I entered contained a rustic, wooden table, as well as a few chairs and an unlit fireplace. On the table, I saw a small book sitting next to a cup of tea from which wafted streams of steam. "What are you reading today?" I asked.

"I'm sure you have heard of Caliburn, the sword that this town, and, by extension, the rest of the country, was founded upon, was stolen by a group of thieves two days ago. In good fashion, I am reading about how it supposedly came to be, and about the warrior who liberated the land we call home today. Why do you ask?" Bertrand seemed ready to answer any question I had for him.

"I was recently admitted into Bastion's corps of mercenaries, and I intend to chase after the thieves that stole the sword."

The confidence in my speech felt unnatural, but I grinned anyway.

"Ah, well, I hope you are well trained in your swordplay! Ogier, First King of the Unified Lands, was the first and last person to wield Caliburn into battle. History tells us that Ogier was quite the swordsman, the best of his time. Through his skills, charisma, and vision, he united the few small city-states and villages around what is now Bastion to become one country, free from foreign oppression. But enough of general history; you learned all of this, I'm sure." I nodded my head. Bertrand sipped on his tea, then proceeded to continue.

"The sword was said to be imbued with supernatural powers…a spirit, you could say. Ogier, in certain legends, was said to have met The Sage. He asked how he could bring peace to his people. The Sage answered: with the sword. The mighty Caliburn felled all who stood in Ogier's way; the purity of his heart led him to retire the sword after founding Bastion and the Unified Lands. Since then, our capital has moved, as you know. But the sword had not. Until a couple of days ago."

I was impressed by how effortlessly Bertrand had compiled all of this information in his head. If Ogier had truly met The Sage, then Caliburn truly was a supernatural weapon, capable in the wrong hands of swathes of chaos. "What do you believe about the sword?" I asked, distraught.

After a few seconds of silence, Bertrand spoke. "As much as I would like to believe some of the myths—I do believe the myths of The Sage, after all—I do not believe that the sword has any supernatural powers. Sometimes items gain power, not from magic, but from the words that surround them. Ogier was recorded as a swordsman without equal before wielding the blade. Caliburn in its construction is not much different from any other sword. Realistically, it has so much value simply because of *who* wielded it and not the other way around. If you fear encountering the thieves, I trust that your skills will lead you to victory against them."

I would not truly know the might of Caliburn without first fighting against it.

"Thank you again, Bertrand.... And what of your own journey? I apologize for not having asked sooner."

Looking at Bertrand's cheerful expression, I knew that he had good news to tell. "Well, friend, after much contemplation, I have decided to join the military!"

I jumped up in excitement. "What made you decide to do that?"

Bertrand grinned. "I was approached by some of Bastion's leading scientists to begin work on a weapon that has recently been brought into development." Bertrand pointed out his window towards a beautiful blue bird. "Such a creation will be able to move through the air as gracefully as that little bird! Aside from its military applications, it will allow people to quickly travel between other countries and even across the world! It will truly be an innovation remembered for centuries, well after I am gone."

I was happy for Bertrand and his new direction in life, but I couldn't help thinking more deeply about what he had said. *It will truly be an innovation remembered for centuries, well after I am gone.* Bertrand knew that his contribution would outlast himself, and that brought a great deal of happiness to his life. Tomorrow, I would be the same as his flying invention: immortal. I attempted to imagine what my life would look like in one hundred years, and then even farther than that.

"You look concerned; is anything bothering you?" Bertrand inquired.

"I snapped out of my daydreaming. "Yes, sorry about that. I was just caught up thinking about how magnificent it would be to fly, like a bird." We both looked at the little blue bird as it flew away.

"And of the girl?" Bertrand asked.

"I haven't seen her in a few days, but we did have a rather interesting time together." I smiled.

"Ah, well, I bet she is just playing coy with you." Bertrand crossed his legs in his seat as he laughed.

Coy was not the word I would use to describe Bella.

"And what of your future spouse?" I jested.

"It was quite refreshing to sit down and talk to such a grounded beauty." Bertrand seemed to melt into his chair, stricken with love.

"No talk of your inventions or your scholarly pursuits?" I inquired.

Bertrand uncrossed his legs and rested his elbow upon the table, stroking his beard slowly. "There is always a time and a place to discuss those things, of course, but I am almost always surrounded by nothing else. It is nice sometimes to talk about less cerebral matters." I nodded my head. "Never forget to talk about sports and the weather on occasion, lest you lose yourself within your own curiosity." Bertrand sipped from his tea cup happily.

"I'll be on my way. Thank you for your hospitality," I said, getting up from my chair.

"Well, friend, I hope that your hunt goes well for you. You truly will be a champion if you reclaim the sword! You too could live on through your accomplishments! I wish you the best of luck!"

I shook Bertrand's hand. "And best of luck to you in your inventing!" Looking into his emerald eyes, I felt an overwhelming sense of calm come over me that I had not felt the first time we met. I wondered if everyone felt the same sort of calm once they figured out what would be truly fulfilling. Leaving Bertrand's house, the calm I had felt quickly dissipated. There was much ahead for me before I would find my true calm.

Colors and sounds were returning to Bastion as I walked down its worn, stone streets: children played as before, and merchants began to display their wares once more. I reached into my bag to look at the warrant for the thieves.

WANTED: DEAD OR ALIVE. FOR THE THEFT OF OUR GREATEST NATIONAL TREASURE, CALIBURN, AND THE MURDER OF 4 SOLDIERS. 3 MEN AND 1 WOMAN. DETAILS WILL BE DISSEMINATED AS MORE INFORMATION BECOMES AVAILABLE. REWARD: 5,000 GOLD PIECES PER THIEF. 10,000 GOLD PIECES FOR RECLAIM-

ING THE SWORD.

I read over the warrant once again to make sure that what I had read was correct. "Five thousand gold pieces for each thief? *Ten* thousand for reclaiming Caliburn? Five thousand is enough for a family to live comfortably for years!" I had known that the rewards would be great, but I hadn't known the exact amounts until now.

As I walked, I overheard two vendors speaking to each other. "Yes! They found the other two thieves dead! They seemed to have been killed at the same time!" I continued eavesdropping as the other man spoke.

"So, the girl is the only one who remains? Whoever found the bodies made a lot of easy money!" I wondered if Raptor and Bone Rattle had already encountered the female thief.

Looking into the sky, clouds continued to move back and forth, causing a blend of blue and gray to pulsate chaotically. The continual shift between colors made me feel uncertain about moving forward to find and defeat the final thief. I knew that I wasn't yet ready. Although I had trained every day since Raptor had gifted me the sword, I wasn't nearly as skilled as he or Rattle. I resolved to visit the tree first, complete my journey, and then think of hunting her down.

I approached the hollow, smiling at how green it all appeared to be. Never was there a moment that I did not take the time to recognize the beauty of nature. I thought back to the point in time when this adventure had started—lying in a lush field, being comforted by the gentle frisks of creation. I continued to walk farther into the hollow, the air becoming cooler and the sky above me obscured by branches.

"That tree...the world around it has grown and changed miraculously." While I thought about how pleasant it had been to take care of the tree, I took a deep breath and closed my eyes happily. When I had opened them again, I couldn't believe what I saw ahead of me. "Raptor! Bone Rattle!" I fell to the ground, yelling at their bodies. Both had been injured, with blood staining the ground around them like puddles after a heavy storm. "Raptor! Bone Rattle!" I called out to both once more. Bone Rattle remained unresponsive, but a gurgle alerted me that Raptor was still alive, to some extent.

"Whelp...come here." Inspecting Raptor closely, I could see that he had lacerations across the entirety of his body. "I gave her a good go at it...if you can see..." Raptor smiled and then coughed up blood, pain ringing throughout his voice.

"What happened? You could never be bested! Raptor..." I began to tear up.

"I have...never encountered such a warrior in my life.... Frederick...pales in comparison to the strength..." Raptor coughed once again.

"Raptor! Please save your energy—I will get you help!" I continued to cry.

"Whelp! I have been ready...for so long now.... Rattle, he is injured...but only unconscious..." I felt a wave of terrible energy overcome the entirety of the hollow.

"Raptor.... I will kill her!" I was overwhelmed. A frenzy of fury coursed through my body.

"Whelp...it is...suicide...do not..."

I could see that Raptor did not have much time left. "Raptor! Your death will not be in vain!"

"You dumb...ha ha ha.... I have rubbed off on you a bit too much.... Your spirit, it burns white hot now like the brilliant arcs of fire that trail through the skies during storms.... Always remain close to what makes your spirit burn this bright.... Have you found it yet? Ah...Whelp...I.... Yes, I know now that I have truly lived...." Raptor let out one last, long breath.

I continued to cry, unnerved and in disbelief. "...Have I found it yet? I don't even know what I am looking for anymore..."

Running towards the tree, I could feel the terrible energy filling the air, making it harder to breathe with each stride I took. Coming upon the tree, a dark figure stood underneath the multitude of branches waving gloomily; even the tree could feel what I was feeling now. "You! Who are you? Why did you steal the sword? You cur—answer me!" The figure turned to me and unveiled her cape, stopping me short. "No.... How...." All that rage that had filled me instantly disappeared.

"Traveler..." she said calmly.

"Why?"

"I never meant to get so close to you. You...you didn't need to meet someone like me," Bella said in a somber tone.

"I just can't understand.... Why did you do this.... Why did you do all of this?" I screamed into the air; my words echoing across the bleak horizon. I could have known it all along, had I not been so willingly deceived by her, an unassuming girl with impressive sword-wielding skills and a propensity for aggression. Bella glanced down and then looked towards me again, unfeelingly.

"Power. You see..." She pulled Caliburn out of her scabbard. Its ancient blade was still covered with blood. "These people, born into a life of easy happiness—they will never truly know the pain I endured. I had no one to love and support me. You, Traveler...you distracted me from the true purpose of my time in Bastion. This sword; its handle is addictive. I have never felt so much power! With such infinite strength resting in my hand, I will be able to subjugate all who oppose me."

Bella's twisted expression frightened me. Her eyes, which had once paralyzed me with love, now did so with fear.

"Bella, do you not remember that day? You seemed so happy! I would have taken care of you! You.... You made me feel emotions I had never felt before!" I yelled out to her, my heart strained, confused from all that had happened today.

"Bah! What emotions do you speak of? I need no taking care of!"

I could see by her face that she was insincere. She continued to speak forcefully. "It is far too late for us, anyway. I am a murderer, and I have stolen what has been rightfully mine for years now. I have suffered through enough pain; I deserve to hold Caliburn until my last breath!"

Her face continued to twist as she spoke. Soon, her mind would be completely warped by the limitless strength loosed by the sword.

"How could I have been so blind? I should have known you were a part of this terrible ordeal…" My lips quivered with anger.

"You were distracted. As was I. I didn't want to find you again after that night we spent together…. Curse destiny for putting you in front of me again!" Bella howled harshly.

"Bella…please listen to me. Return the sword. It is not too late for you, or for us. There is light in your heart, I know there is. Don't forsake the rest of your life, please…" I looked into her eyes again, hoping to see just a glimmer of what I had seen in them before.

"And what then, Traveler? Do not be so foolish as to believe there is any other option for me! What we shared between us, it did feel nice, but it is gone now. Please…leave."

Her gaze emanated darkness; her soul had lost that element which keeps most from venturing too deep into the haze of malevolence.

"Bella. Return the sword." I gripped the hilt of my sword tightly, praying I would not have to utilize everything I had learned in order to wrest the sword from the shadow standing in place of someone I had loved so much.

"Ah, yes! You mean to take Caliburn from me, then? Leave this place at once—I do not wish to hurt you."

Bella assumed her fighting stance, and I was taken aback by the sheer power that resonated from the blade.

This could be it. You could run from this place. No one would judge you a coward. No one would expect any more out of you. Why sacrifice your journey now? Tomorrow, you will live the rest of eternity peacefully.

It was true. If I fled now, I would not be a coward. After word of Raptor's death, all would know how fearsome an enemy Bella would be. How could I think I would ever be capable of defeating any of the thieves? Especially the one wielding the most supreme weapon of our times? I quivered, discouraged at the truth of the situation.

"And you believe that?" Now, the cat inside me was speak-

ing—roaring courageously. "Before this week, you had done nothing that separated one day from the next. Now, you are at the
pinnacle of your adventure! There are so many people who count
on you right now to at least try and reclaim Caliburn! And if you
die? You will live on as the boy who faced off against the strongest warrior alive! And if you win? You will be forever known as
the boy who, against all odds, *defeated* the strongest warrior alive!
Our story could very well end today, but *what a story it would be!*"

I thought first about what my mind said and then what
my instincts said: *Remain in tune with the instincts that have always resided within you, and the path you must travel will become
clear.* Frederick had said that when we do not trust ourselves, we
leave room for mistakes and errors. I inhaled more deeply than I
ever had before. The air around my scabbard hissed as I drew my
sword. Our fates would be the result of one final dance of steel and
dreams.

I advanced forward, reaching into my bag to grab the jar
of water. I poured the contents of the jar onto the ground and
watched as the water seeped into earth. Looking up, the tree
began to grow and shift slowly.

"I give you one final warning. You were lucky to beat me
the first time we met. There will be no luck if you dare try me
again." Bella exuded a monstrous air, one so fearsome I couldn't
help but shudder at its might. I drove my boots into the ground
and locked eyes with Bella.

"I know who I met that day; I know you are still in there
somewhere!" I shouted.

"You are so full of hope—and for what? Those rotten vermin that helped me steal Caliburn? I gave them hope! I gave
them hope that riches awaited them, and their hope led them to
their demise. The mercenaries? I do owe one of them for saving
me from those wretched city streets, but even he left me after
a while! The other was a formidable opponent but not nearly
the adversary I had hoped to face. You said something about
him before...Merciless Eagle...? An intimidating title for such a
weak warrior." My knuckles cracked from clutching my sword so

tightly. "In my hands, I hold an infinite amount of power. Power. *That* is what rules this world and nothing else!"

Every moment I had lived had brought me to this point in time, this terrible point over which I had no control: I was being pushed off the cliff of violence and into an uncertain darkness.

I ran forward and swung my sword at Bella. The tree grew larger than any other I had seen; the sky could have been completely cradled by its massive limbs. Before our swords could connect, Bella seemed to vanish like a wraith. The speed she had gained from Caliburn astonished me. *And I thought she was fast before.*

I dodged quickly out of the way of one of her strikes. The amount of force behind her blow caused a shockwave that sent me across the field like a dandelion seed blown by the wind. "Leave this place at once! You are far too weak to stand a chance against me!" Bella yelled.

"Stand a chance against you? You have done nothing! It's the sword you wield!" I retorted. I could feel my spirit scorch and blaze as I got up from the ground. "You aren't worthy to hold Caliburn in your hands! A noble soul held that sword before you, and he used the vast amounts of power presented to him to liberate those he cared about. You use the same power for selfish purposes —your only wish is to subdue the world around you! Can you not see how *twisted* you have become?" I roared.

"What would you understand about my goals, Traveler? I learned early on that only the strongest among us to get to experience the highest fruits that life has to offer. The rest are left to feed from the slops. Caliburn will give me what I have sought for so long...kneel before me!" Bella pressed Caliburn into the ground, sending a burst of energy through the earth that caused me to fall over easily. "Look at you! How could you ever think you could defeat me now!"

I shook my head in disappointment. "I don't wish to defeat you, Bella. My only wish is that you come back to me the way you were before."

I got up from the ground once again, regaining my composure before Bella could strike again.

"That person you met...she no longer exists. Traveler... please...you're causing me to doubt myself. I do not wish to hurt you." Her voice softened for just a few moments.

"Bella! I know you can change your path! Please..." I felt like a root was being pulled, angrily, out of my heart. I had imagined so much on the day I had met her. No one had ever made me so happy. Our situation now seemed like a terrible nightmare, come to life.

"I am poisonous, can't you see? If you continue to fight me here, I will show you no quarter. *Go!*"

"Show no quarter then!" I attacked her once more, pouring the entirety of my soul into each of my blows.

"Aaagh!" Bella yelled in agony as I caught her forearm with my blade.

"Release the sword! It was never yours to wield!" I was completely in tune with my instincts at this point, letting go of control and channeling everything that I had predicted through all my swings.

"This is it! Become another victim of my might!" Bella growled like a feral animal cornered in a cage.

I worked to dodge and parry the seemingly infinite torrent of blows that now struck from every direction. "Why do you not fear me? You behave like that stupid mercenary!" I truly feared for my life at this point, but the cat's power drove me to subdue my fears and fight desperately to the end. I could feel aches from my side and my other injuries, but my perturbation over all that had happened fueled a primal need to persist.

In a single moment, she left herself open in her rage.

"Urgh!" Bella grunted and winced painfully, as I left a small gash in her arm.

"Will you...not quit yet?" I asked her, attempting to regain my breath between words. Blood ran from her arms like ink, writing a gruesome story onto the grass below us.

"Never! How have you lasted this long against me? I am the most powerful warrior alive!"

Hope, I thought.

Bella came at me once again. This contest was no longer fought between bodies but souls. As we clashed, I could feel our spirits burn like two stars in the night sky. Parrying one of many blows that rained upon me, my sword began to crack. As I looked in disbelief at my blade, it shattered to pieces like fragile glass.

"You fool! I have destroyed that pathetic little dagger you called a sword!" Bella laughed sadistically. "Now fall to me!"

Her final swing sent a blast in my direction that threw me off into the distance into one of the trees that surrounded us. I hit the tree with excessive force, my body ringing with indescribable pain. My vision became blurry. "Bella..." As I blinked my eyes, it became harder to remain conscious. In my final blinks, I saw Bella run from our improvised battlefield. "Aagh! Bella..." I laid motionless on the ground; my vision was filled with a dull white.

I didn't know how much later, but something poked me with force, and I heard Bone Rattle's voice. "Are you alive, little house cat?"

"Rattle!" In my excitement, I threw my arms around him, forgetting how much pain I was in. "Ow! I'm excited that you are alive!" My smile quickly dissipated when I remembered who wasn't with us anymore.

"No, ol' Bone Rattle isn't truly a pile of rattling bones just yet. Raptor...that damned fool."

"Rattle, Bella said that you were the person who saved her from the street, years ago." Bone Rattle looked confused, then exasperated.

"That girl! I remember her.... I've always loved money, and before I met Raptor, I was a grand sailor, terrorizing pirates for the benefit of those in the harbor towns—for profit, of course. After a hard day's work, I would make my way to the local tavern. If you had seen her eyes in that alleyway, those sad eyes just begging for help, you would have done the same thing! But as for taking care... a hungry shark could have taken better care of her than I could! So I brought her to an orphanage. Better for her to be there than to die in some filthy gutter. That girl...she was just a puppy in the streets. How did she come to this?" Bone Rattle's eyes dripped tears as his demeanor grew more and more sorrowful.

"Rattle, we should bring Raptor's body back to town and see to it that he has a proper—" Bone Rattle cut me off before I could finish talking.

"He always said if it ever came down to this, he would want to be cast upon the pyre, his body then blown by the wind in as many directions as it would take him." I nodded in agreement. "Let's get a move on, house cat. Let's get this old eagle to town..." Rattle and I limped through the hollow, hoisting Raptor's body across our shoulders along the way.

Frederick hastily organized a funeral ceremony, ordering a pyre constructed in order to comply with what Raptor had wanted. The cool of the night helped soothe the pain of my wounds but not the pain I felt, having lost two people I had cared about so passionately. Bone Rattle and I sat in a row next to a few other mercenaries. Altogether, 20 or so people gathered to pay their respects to the Merciless Eagle.

"Ah, perk up, will ye? For now, we are safe. That Frederick is going on and on as he usually does.... A 'few words' from him, and we will be dead, too, by the time he stops talking!" Bone Rattle cackled away silently. I grinned, but his humor could not stop my ruminations. I thought about Bella—where she was and what she intended to do with Caliburn.

"Appearances, Adventurer. Do not be deceived by them."

My mind was pervaded with too many conflicting thoughts to pay attention to most of what Frederick was talking about. I thought back to what The Sage had said so many days ago. Bella had been so sweet when I had first met her, but she had also been infinitely mysterious. In her struggles, Bella's deepest desire had become power. I was but a distraction from what she truly wanted the most. And yet: *Maybe she fooled herself. Maybe what she really wanted is love*, I thought with a flickering hope.

"...And so, we sit here, illuminated only by the fires that burn before us. Raptor, as he chose to be called, dedicated the latter part of his life to stopping those who spread fear and chaos across the land. All we can do now is continue where Raptor has fallen. His life served as a true testament to the ability we have to change our lives for the better. We go forth now, remembering that we, too, may always change and continuing to build up the fire that he has started. Thank you all, and best of luck in your hunts."

Frederick turned and gazed at the fire, his face stoic even in such solemn times.

Lightning, while fleeting, is exciting. It burns gloriously and leaves all who see it amazed, stupefied, even, I remembered him saying. *You succeeded,* I told him silently, watching the flames burn until there was nothing left but smoldering ash. I hoped that, one day, someone would look up to me the way I had looked up to Raptor.

Everyone else had left the ceremony except for Frederick, Bone Rattle, and I. "Boy, come here for a few minutes," Frederick called. "Bone Rattle told me about Ogier's sword, but I am sure you have also seen its capabilities for yourself. The girl remains a threat, not only to our people, but to the world at large. I never knew that old piece of steel contained so much power...and neither does anyone else. I ask you to remain quiet about the whole affair until we can figure out a way to defeat her and reclaim the sword for The Stronghold."

I agreed.

"And what of your sword?" Frederick asked, glancing at my scabbard curiously.

"In my duel with the girl, it shattered to pieces." Frederick, startled, reached under the podium to grab something. "Here. I am sure you are familiar with this blade. Raptor's belongings had no specified recipient, and, after discussing with Bone Rattle, we decided that they should all go to you."

Stunned, I bowed to Frederick and shook Bone Rattle's hand firmly. "Thank you all.... I never anticipated my life bringing me here."

Frederick looked at me proudly. "Boy, limitless potential resides within you. While much can change during your life, that will not. Go and rest—we will discuss more tomorrow."

Leaving the pyre, I wrapped my fingers around the hilt of Raptor's sword. "This whelp won't let you down," I said, to Raptor and to myself. Looking upon Raptor's ashes once more as I walked away, I knew that he had left this world the way he had wished.

One last day, and my journey would be over. Eternal life would be mine at last, and, with it, I would wrench Death's hold from my life permanently.

On this sullen day, I had lost so much. All I wanted now was the answer. My answer.

I spoke out loud to The Sage, wherever he was. "Give me what I have been chasing. I know I have proved my worth to you."

DAY 7:

THE SAGE'S SECRET

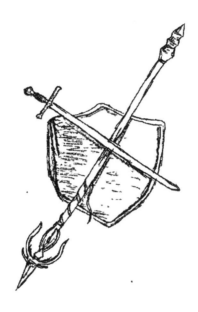

I stood in the middle of the town square, listening to the fountain's flow and looking into the distance. From Raptor, I had inherited a thousand gold pieces, enough money to last for months, even with profligate spending. His sword was of a heftier build than my previous one but not uncomfortable. With my eyes closed, I took in the serenity that floated through the town. Today was the last day that I would go visit the tree; this was as exciting as it was sorrowful.

I decided not to waste any time, and I ran through the forest, noticing nothing but where The Sage's cottage had stood seven days ago. *I will see you again soon enough.*

Exiting the forest, I walked down the road to Bastion, seeing the usual flow of people traveling to and from different towns. Reaching the gate, I noticed a different guard. He was not slouchy and sluggish like the last soldier. I realized he was the soldier that had attacked me earlier in the week.

"State your business in our—well met! Sorry I did not recognize you sooner." The young man seemed oddly ecstatic to see me.

"Well met, soldier. I am just passing through today." The only thought on my mind was tending to the tree one last time and then sprinting back to The Sage's cottage.

"I apologize for what I did the other day. It was foolish of me to act on such powerful emotions. If my brother had seen my behavior, he would have scolded me to no end. As punishment, I have been moved to guard duty for a few months. Frederick told me that you fought my brother's killer the other day. Are all the legends surrounding that old sword true?"

I met the young soldier's eyes. "I've nothing to say about that."

He looked back at me despondently. "In any case, I wish you the best of luck, warrior."

We shook hands. After walking away from him, I couldn't help but let a small grin spread across my face. "Warrior, huh?" I murmured. "I have a lot of work ahead of me before I will truly earn that title."

Seeing colorful and loud children playing in Bastion's monochromatic streets rose my spirits but contemplation about the sword continued to be at the forefront of my mind. Raptor and Bella had both lost their lives to that sword—the former, physically, and the latter, spiritually. If what Bertrand had said was true, The Sage picked Ogier centuries ago for his noble soul, for such power should only be wielded by someone with a pure heart. All these days later, I was still suspect as to why The Sage had picked *me*. Ogier had been a great man, both in his character and in his accomplishments. I was not.

WANTED: DEAD OR ALIVE. THIEF WHO STOLE OUR GREATEST NATIONAL TREASURE, CALIBURN. THIEF IS

KNOWN BY THE NAME "BELLADONNA." 15,000 GOLD PIECE-REWARD FOR RECLAMATION OF SWORD AND HER CAPTURE OR EXECUTION.

The city was covered in these posters, promising an exorbitant amount of gold pieces to any mercenary or soldier who could catch Bella and retrieve the sword. I cringed at the thought of any more people meeting their ends the way Raptor had. After seeing a glimpse of what Bella was now capable of, I knew that even an entire army would have a difficult time standing against her.

I had reached the outskirts of Bastion; my heart raced as I stood at the city's edge. Beyond the hollow lay a reward far greater than any fame or fortune. I tromped through, proud that I had made it this far and thinking of the centuries to come. With so much time, I could travel the world, never having to conclude my vagabond state. As I neared the tree, I noticed an overgrowth of plants and flowers where Raptor had fallen yesterday. "Maybe the tree did this...you didn't pass without making an impact, Eagle." I hoped that his ashes would see parts of the world he never had and that those ashes would bring new life to the grounds upon which they fell.

As I came upon the entrance to the tree's birthplace, I was forced by a flash of overwhelming light to stop and cover my eyes.

An unearthly, feminine voice spoke to me in an eerily calm tone: "Adventurer...this is the last day you will have to visit this secluded grove."

Opening my eyes, a suit of disorienting ivory armor stood in front of me, the same suit of armor that had spooked me in The Sage's cottage. The helmet was composed of two faces—one, a fledgling soldier; the other, a battle-hardened veteran.

"Janus! I didn't know you could speak! What are you doing here?"

He had an ethereal nature and an unnerving, unchanging gaze, lit by an azure spark in each eye. "I am the master of all gateways, Adventurer. I was present at the entrance to your quest, and I am present now at its egress. Tell me, do you recognize this person?" In the reflection of his armor, I saw a boy full of hope but devoid of bravery; who despised ignorance but had not yet seen the power of knowledge; who knew nothing of love; who had not yet persevered; who had not yet found his duty to himself; who was blind to the continual flux of the universe. A boy who had not once chased after something that truly invigorated his soul.

"Now look," Janus said.

In an instant, the image before me changed. This boy exuded courage, comprehension, passion, indefatigability, loyalty, plasticity, and a zealous determination.

"Adventurer, you have done well over the last week, but now—" I had thought that he was here to congratulate me, but now I was not so sure. I hopped back as the air around Janus' hand began to crackle and glow. "—you must show me what you have learned."

His spear began to materialize within the faint azure glow that floated through the air.

"Janus! You don't mean..."

It all felt like one big joke, but as I stared into Janus' emotionless helmet, I knew this was truly my final trial.

"Ascalon, the Dragon Slayer. Caliburn's complement in might and eminence." Janus put the butt of his ornate spear into the ground as his shield materialized out of thin air. "This spear.... You failed to acquire the only weapon that could match its prowess." Janus' otherworldly voice echoed throughout the tree's birthplace.

"Caliburn."

"I loaned someone that sword long ago...recently, it fell into less capable hands. Nonetheless..." Blue energy sparked throughout the air once more, and in a flash of light, there it was: Caliburn. "I reclaimed what has been mine for centuries."

I was astonished and worried. "Janus! What did you do to Bella?" I shouted.

"The girl is fine. She would not give up the blade by choice, so we had a duel. Quite adept with a sword she was.... Not adept enough to defeat me, though. The power contained within Caliburn would drive her selfish mind mad. I only hope that she learned a lesson through our short, yet riveting, encounter."

Caliburn floated in front of me, its humble hilt beckoning.

"You will not stand a chance if you face me with the sword you have now. Take Caliburn and fight," Janus instructed, entirely devoid of emotion.

I looked at the tree, and then shifted my eyes towards Janus' gaze, my fingers slowly wrapping around Caliburn's time-worn handle. Incredible power surged throughout my body. The only obstacle now was Janus, the gatekeeper to the infinite realm. "Now, Adventurer. What have you learned?"

I hoped that, through my swordplay, I could offer an acceptable answer.

A tremendous amount of fortitude was transferred from the blade and into my mind. Every trial I had come across had required a blind, reckless courage, and now was no exception. With the might of what felt like a god, I swung Caliburn and loosed a shockwave that rattled through the hollow. Janus held his shield to the blast, and I watched in awe as the shockwave fell away almost instantly.

Ascalon blazed with the same sort of energy as Caliburn. I tried to block one of Janus' fierce stabs, but his proficiency with the spear was too great. It was apparent why Bella had lost her swift encounter with the armor. Knocked to the ground, I rolled out of the way to avoid being stabbed.

"Agh!" I yelled out, as I felt the cold spear bore into my arm. I had been extremely averse to any sort of danger before beginning my travels to the tree; now it was as if the goddess of peril wished to have her way with me.

"This spear has slain the mightiest of dragons. It will have no problem defeating you if you let it."

Looking at the expressionless face above me, I remembered my mother and those whom I had met on my journey. I could not afford to fall here today.

Janus released his spear from my arm, leaving a gaping wound. I sprang up, feeling blood drip down to my fingertips. Running towards Janus furiously, the overwhelming desire to succeed veiled all the pain I had felt moments before. Swinging into Janus' spear, I could see reality bend and warp before my eyes. "Gah!" I screamed, his spear going deeply into one of my shoulders. He pulled the spear out again, and I began to whimper and grimace in agony. My body was growing weaker, the lifeforce draining out of me as I lost more of myself to the battle and to the ground. I used all I had left in me to keep fighting. We traded an innumerable number of stabs and slashes, both of us unwilling to concede any opportunities to the other.

"You do not quit. Why?" Janus stopped as his spear faded back into nothing.

I also stopped, feeling the injuries I had sustained seal up miraculously.

"Eternal life," I said simply, though it seemed obvious to me why I had not quit. Since I had met The Sage, I had had many opportunities to do so. The prize that awaited me was simply far too valuable.

"You were mortally wounded, and yet you continued to fight. If we had finished our duel, I surely would have killed you. Yet you continued to fight. Even holding one of the mightiest weapons in the universe, you were afraid. Yet you continued to fight." Janus stood in front of the tree, then began to fade away, just as Ascalon had moments earlier.

"Janus?" I wondered what the purpose of our encounter had been—if there had been a purpose at all. His ethereal voice echoed around me.

"You thought I was here to test your swordsmanship, or your resolve, but that is not the case. I, as the master of the gates, will share with you a secret: you alone decide your beginning and your end. To start, you must end, and to end, you must start. In between those two points, *that* is what you have learned...and so I ask you again. What have you learned?" By the time he finished speaking, Janus had disappeared altogether.

"What have I learned...?" I tried to divine what Janus meant, but I could not find an answer now.

Light filled the tree's birthplace as I finished pouring out the last of the water from my jar. When I looked up, a familiar sight caused a smile to spread across my face.

"Finally," I sighed.

I brushed the verdant moss that lined the entirety of The Sage's door. Knocking, I could feel my heartbeat intensify. After a few moments, it opened.

"Come in." The Sage's powerful voice rumbled as I entered his domain once more. "So." His ocean-blue robe flowed gracefully around him as he closed the door behind me. "Seven days. Seven days is a long time when you have to wait for something, don't you think?"

What he said may have been true at first, but the constant stream of new experiences that I had encountered had helped pass the time rather significantly. "Well, you know..."

The Sage began to speak before I could finish my sentence. "You have seen a great deal of what the world has to offer. Walk with me."

Vaguely irritated by his interruption, I followed his lead, delving farther into his immeasurable realm.

The hallways of the cottage stretched on as we walked to an unspecified destination. "You picked up a few new items along your travels, I see." I nodded. "I haven't seen that sword in centuries. That used to be Janus' favorite, until he acquired that toothpick he carries around all the time. How do you like it?"

I did not know how to answer. Although I felt infinitely powerful wielding Caliburn, I had no interest in keeping it any longer than I needed to.

The Sage motioned towards one of the chairs. My bottom felt uncomfortable on the hard wooden seat. "You have solidified your place in history. Tales of your heroism in reclaiming the sword will be told for centuries. Return Caliburn to Bastion, and you will live on forever, after your passing as a hero."

I looked at him harshly, unsatisfied. "So this is it? Maybe you misunderstood me when I asked you for eternal life."

"No, I understood you perfectly. You have completed your quest and achieved something that most people never do."

I felt as if I had been tricked—I never wished to be a hero or be remembered. My question six days earlier had been a simple one: *how does one gain eternal life*? "Sage, I know you are withholding something from me." I stood up and set my hands on the table forcefully. With a pained glance, The Sage looked at me for a few moments.

"Maybe it is time for me to tell you my secret, then, Adventurer." He sighed and shook his head slowly. "Silly boy...why do you wish to live forever? Really think about it before you answer me."

I sat back in my chair, a floral scent billowing from the teacups. What I knew intuitively was that living forever would allow me to do as I pleased until time itself came to a halt. There was nothing I had ever wanted more. Why would The Sage withhold that from me?

"You know, Adventurer, I like you. You remind me of myself when I was your age. I will not play coy with you. The sort of power that lies within that sword would drive most people mad. Not you, obviously."

I felt the handle of the sword and thought of Bella. After all the misfortune and pain in her early life, power had become her only perceived solution. The more I thought of our two encounters, the more I despaired for her.

"The girl is safe, to put your mind at ease." I whipped my head around to look into his eyes. "Love is fickle, Adventurer. You loved the girl and she loved you, but your paths were as destined to intersect as they were to diverge again. That, more often than not, is the nature of reality." I opened my mouth to speak and then decided to remain silent. The deep-red carpets that covered the floors were beginning to become disorienting, as the pale gold walls of each hallway swirled and shifted.

"Here we are." The Sage opened the door in front of us.

Grass started where the carpet ended, and as I investigated the room, what I had worked so hard to visit every day lay in the middle of the clearing. A quaint table sat under its multitude of branches.

"I prepared some different tea today that I thought you might like." The Sage smiled.

"How did you do this?"

"Do what? My tiny home has many rooms; I couldn't have been bothered to show you all of them the first time you visited."

I scowled slightly. The Sage's sense of humor could truly only be appreciated by an animated suit of armor—as a matter of fact, Janus seemed to become frustrated by his jests as often as I did.

"Adventurer, take a seat." I sat. "Before you answer my question, let me entertain you with a story that may sway you in another direction." The Sage held the intricate teacup in his hands as if he was going to take a sip and then set the cup back on the table. "I was a boy like you once—a boy whose curiosity could not be sated. At this point, I had completed my schooling, and I knew that there were too many adventures to be had and not enough time in which to have them. There was a myth of a fellow who knew the answer to every question, and if you had a question you simply could not go to the grave without have answered, he would answer it for you.

"In my travels, I came across this quaint little house and its previous owner the same way you did and was just as baffled by it, and by him. The fellow who lived here sent me on a few errands before he would give me my answer; he was far too old. The Sage and Janus became my closest friends. No one knew them the way I did; to everyone else, they were tales out of a storybook. As the years passed, The Sage became sick, and his body could not bear to live another day.

"'Mark,' he coughed sullenly. 'I will breathe my last in just a few moments. You have been a dear friend to me, and I apologize for giving you what you had always wanted.'

"I held his cold, pale hands in genuine confusion as he passed into the ether.

"Then, the years began to pass. I had fallen in love, and with her and a gallery of unmatched companions, I continued my travels. But soon, time took all of them. One by one, everyone I loved was dragged into the same ether into which The Sage had disappeared. Even my wife, as enduring as she was, succumbed in the end. I looked at my hands, at my face—I had not aged since the fateful day when I had completed my final errand for the old man. I had seen so much and had done everything I had ever wanted to do, and my soul was sated.

"But time continued to move on.

"I came back to this house and began to explore it more thoroughly than I had before. My only wish now was to find something—anything—that would help me understand it all. Janus spoke of a fruit The Sage had come across in his own travels, one that would grant its consumer infinite knowledge. I came across that fruit myself and ate it—if I had to live forever, I at least wanted to be able to make sense of what I had gotten myself into.

"Immediately upon eating, I began to laugh. I had become wise to the world, but the answer still eluded me. Days, months, years, centuries, millennia.... I still do not know why I ever wanted to live forever. My time as The Sage started when I decided to use my newfound illimitable knowledge as my predecessor had. I presented myself to many interesting and virtuous souls, all of whom went on to live the lives they truly wanted. Even with finite knowledge and wisdom, I was powerless to make a meaningful dent in the history of the universe. But in helping others—that is what truly gave my existence meaning again."

I looked at The Sage in silence.

"I have rambled. I have given you your eternal life. You are free to stay if you—"

Anger built up in my heart. The last sage had not been a charlatan like this one, surely. I had never wished to become a hero, nor had I wished to become a piece of history. My only wish had been for my heart to never beat its last. I had spilled my blood and put up my life to secure my immortality; what The Sage spoke of was not the outcome I had expected.

"You gave me the job of planting this silly tree and taking care of it for the last seven days. I did it. I risked my life at times for that tree...all to provide some bower for you and your afternoon tea? I've my own life to live, a life that will be quite different from yours. Give me what I came here for," I growled.

"So, you have divined no meaning from your successes. Are you blind to all you have seen thus far? I promise you, what I have given is better than what you expected to receive. You will live on in the minds of others. Stories of your exploits will be told for generations! You have had such an impact on so many, and you still have so much to do! Are you so blind as to not see all that?"

I slammed my hands on the table and stood up abruptly.

"I read those old myths and for a while, you tricked me into believing they were true, but now I know that they really are what everyone has made them out to be. You identify as The Sage, but you are just an old man, trapped within his own insecurities. If you know so much, what happens next? Where do I go now?"

The Sage remained silent as he looked up at me.

"There was no purpose to any of this, then," I concluded. "That is what you saw all those days ago, you deluded me! To you, this was all a game—to watch some boy scurry back and forth for your amusement!"

"What you truly want is all up to you now. I have nothing more to say to you." The Sage sipped from his teacup and looked off into the distance.

"You were right; you are a lot like me. You are just as blind to what goes on in this world as I am."

"I will leave then, if we have nothing more to discuss."

In silence, The Sage got up from his chair and walked away, the door disappearing as it shut behind him.

"What was the purpose of it all?" I muttered, slumping down next to the tree. The hilts of both Caliburn and Raptor's sword dug into my waist, and I sighed softly. I regretted losing my temper. The one lesson he had wished me to learn was patience, and I had not even gotten that.

The sun was warm on my skin as I looked into the distance.

Maybe The Sage had a point; if anything, I would never have seen so much, had I not been tasked with caring for the tree.

Seven days ago, I met a figure who would change my life forever. Seven days ago, I truly began to live. Seven days ago, my life became a story worth telling.

Was there really any reason to live forever?

Seven days ago, I had been certain there was. Now, I wasn't so sure.

DAY 8:

HALL OF MIRRORS

"Slowpoke! You never told me I was training a hero!"

Helene's cheerful voice was instantly recognizable among the crowd of people celebrating in the streets. Returning Caliburn to Bastion had caused the town to erupt with a new sort of life and happiness I had not seen before. I had declined the award offered by the city, asking that it be used instead to help people like my mother prosper for years to come.

"Helene! I did not know you were training a hero, either!" I laughed as shook hands.

"This means that I will have to train you from now on, to ensure that you are ready to conquer even bigger challenges!"

I smiled and nodded happily.

"I see there is a medal around your neck; where is that from?" I inquired.

"Well, I wasn't planning on competing again so soon, but something about seeing you train excited me enough to race this morning. It was tough, but I am the champion! I even broke a few records!"

"Congratulations! That is wonderful!" I patted Helene on the shoulder. Seeing her jubilant smile, I thought back to The Sage: *Maybe she was more deserving of one of your secrets.*

I felt bad after the previous day's meeting—I had overreacted, and I might not ever be able to apologize.

"Are you okay?" Helene asked, noticing the sudden change in my demeanor.

"I am, just wondering what I should do now."

Helene scratched her head and then jumped up excitedly. "There is always going to be another race to run! This is only the beginning of all the great things you can accomplish!"

I smiled, knowing that what she said was true. Although I had not acquired eternal life, at least by what I had imagined it to be, I knew that there was still plenty of more life for me to have. "Thank you, Helene. I wish you the best in all of your future endeavors."

Saying goodbye, I was grabbed forcefully by the shoulders. "Housecat! I was thinking hard the other day...of course, with old Eagle being gone, I'll be needing a new partner. All the other mercenaries seem too cowardly to take on the sort of warrants Raptor and I used to chase after. Squirrel had offered to move to Bastion, but you know just as well as I that the tree hopper would never tolerate my alcoholic tendencies.... And I do still owe him quite a sum of money. You seem to have put on quite a bit of bravery, or stupidly, since we had first met. I'll let you think it over, but if you wish to make a career out of being a soldier of fortune, it is open to you." Bone Rattle's rickety giggles belied the true severity of his offer.

I had been thinking about learning a trade or becoming a merchant before my travels to the tree, but now mercenary work seemed to be the only option that truly excited me. "I will definitely think about it, Rattle. Until then, stay alive! I will be disappointed if you ever become a true pile of rotting bones." Rattle patted me on the head; I scowled and then laughed.

"You think about it hard; it could be quite lucrative, you know."

As he walked away, I thought about how both he and Raptor saved my life. I still owed both of them a huge debt for that.

My mother then surprised me, coming out of the crowd of people. "Son, I am so proud of you for what you have accomplished! I had no idea that this is what you have been doing over the last week!"

"Mother! How did you make it all this way?" I felt a little embarrassed, not having told my mother about my whereabouts, but it seemed not to matter now.

"I was on my way to the gardens, and Helene was running about as she likes to do, and we bumped into each other. She told me that *you* were the one who reclaimed Caliburn for Bastion! I had heard about all that was going on here, but I would never have guessed that you were the hero!" My mother let a few happy tears fall from her eyes as she gave me a hug.

"It all just sort of happened. I never really expected to do anything like this." I looked at her while thinking about all that had occurred in the past week.

"Son, just know that while I value your safety and your life above all else, I've always wanted you to do what feels right." My mother nodded her head firmly.

"I would never wish to cause you any worry," I said, looking down and feeling even more childish now.

"Look at you, you warrior! Here you are with that big sword by your side, and that gruff look on your face…. You even have a few whiskers coming through!" My mother laughed happily. It occurred to me that, while I still felt like the boy who had set out to plant the tree all those days ago, all the people in the crowds—my friends, my mother, the townspeople—were seeing the person I had become.

"Mother…I am just glad I could make you proud."

"It was hard losing your father…. I just know he would be so proud of you now, as I am. Never forget to be proud of yourself. No matter what you decide to do, your father never did, and I never will, stop loving you. You have really grown up to be more than we could have ever thought." My mother stopped and looked at me for a few moments.

"You enjoy the celebration! I will go home with Helene. I love you, my potato!" My mother gave me another hug, and I smiled, embarrassed by her nickname for me.

I looked out into the cheering crowd, waved, and felt an incompleteness come over me.

After the huge celebration had ended, and Frederick had given one of his notoriously long, yet eloquent speeches, I left the city once more to tend that which had become a symbol for this new chapter of my life. The hollow seemed to reflect a beautiful green light into the world as the sun began to set. As I walked, I remembered all those people whom I had met each day.

Janus' words came to me again—"In between those two points, that is what you have learned...and so I ask you again, what have you learned?"

During my excursions to and from the tree, I had met a mercenary whose intimidating demeanor could only be matched by the size of his heart.

I had met a scholar who was much more than just an intelligent savant.

I had met a girl with whom I had fallen in love, only to learn that not everyone is what they seem and that nothing lasts forever.

I had met a runner who was so fast that even her dreams could not elude her.

I had met a proud wolf whose pride resided not within himself, but within his service to others.

A suit of armor had guided me to deeply analyze all that occurs between the gates of beginning and end.

Finally, in meeting a myth, I had learned that not even those who know everything have all the answers.

In this delightful stroll to the tree, I found I had entered a hall of mirrors. Looking at that which had consumed so much of my curiosity over the last week, I was compelled to look deep within myself. To my pleasure, I saw all of the auspicious opportunities I had been afforded.

By the tree still sat the table, chairs, teapot, and cups that had been there yesterday. I walked under the brilliant branches that now enveloped this grove and took a seat at the table, pulling out the jar in my bag to water the tree.

"It has been a pleasure coming to visit you this last week. You have grown to be so large and robust. I hope that we may continue our meetings as time progresses." I opened the jar, pouring all the water out close to the tree. Smiling, I sat back in the chair and poured the rest of the tea from the pot. Surprisingly, it was still warm.

As I sat, enjoying the tea and watching the light of the sun shine across the land, one of the tree's branches began to descend towards the table. It loomed closer, and I saw the branch, like a hand, clenching a small iridescent fruit within its grasp. In the gentlest way, the tree handed me the fruit. I looked at it curiously. My gaze slowly moved towards tree, and I suddenly realized what sat in my hands.

I felt a sort of startling infinity rise out of the golden orb now resting in my palm.

Looking at the fruit again, I knew what I had wanted all along.

About the Author

Angel Santiago is an author, writer, and poet from Neptune, New Jersey raised in the mountains of Southwest Virginia.

Santiago started his writing journey on the website Quora.com, where he has amassed over 2 million views writing about different topics: primarily History and Philosophy. He was given a Top Writer Award by the website in 2018.

When he is not writing books, answering questions on Quora, or sharing his haikus and poetry on Instagram, Santiago enjoys spending time with friends and family as well as reading.

Made in the USA
Columbia, SC
29 August 2021